VIVIAN, MIDNIGHT CALL GIRL

IRON ORCHIDS

DANIELLE NORMAN

VIVIAN, MIDNIGHT CALL GIRL

Drunk dialing at it's finest...

All it took was a couple bottles of champagne...
And a fully charged cellphone,
For me to go from widow to call girl.
Talking to a stranger in the middle of the night was the push
I needed.
To feel something again.
Something safe.

It's not like I will ever run into him.
We don't even know each other... yet.
Aaron Skye returns my call the next day,
Sending my well-ordered world for a spin.
Now I'm sober.

After years in the shadows,
I'm starting to feel alive. A sense of normalcy.
Unfortunately Aaron is not who I had imagined.
And his life is anything but normal.

Can I put the phone down and step into his world long
enough to realize,
That what started out as careless whispers has smoldered
into something more?
A wrong number, could be my Mr. Right.

This is dedicated to all the fucking authors who find it fun and easy to write sex scenes.

FYI, I dislike you big time, I mean huge, gigantic (and there is no jealousy there, lol).

Especially Elle Christensen who steps in to save my deplorable stick-it-in-wham-bam-thank-you-mam sex scenes.

I think Amish Romance is calling my name...hmmm?

"Wrinkles will only go where the smiles have been"
— Jimmy Buffet

PROLOGUE

VIVIAN

 our years ago . . .

"Don't get up, baby." Eric leaned over to kiss me. "Today you have got to make a decision about where you want to go. Honey, we are less than six months away from our five-year wedding anniversary, and I don't want to spend it here."

"I know, I know. I promise," I said as I leaned up to meet him halfway. Eric and I had been high school sweethearts, even though he was two years older. Even when he went off to college, he came home every weekend to see me. Our love was a forever type of love; sometimes I had to pinch myself to prove that this was my life and not some dream. "Can I make you something to eat before you go into work?"

"Sleep, I've got it." Eric kissed me again. "I love you." The smell of Irish Spring soap lingered even after he pulled away.

"Love you too. Be safe."

Eric paused in the open doorway of our bedroom. "Always."

I closed my eyes and nestled back into my warm covers to get a few more hours of shut-eye. Sliding one hand over to his pillow, I squeezed it and then tucked it under my chin. The cold cotton was soothing as I fell back to sleep.

I sat straight up to the sound of my doorbell and then glanced at the clock on my nightstand. Shit, it was after nine.

I jumped out of bed just as my doorbell rang again. "I'm coming." I raced through the house as I finger-combed my hair. I pulled open the door and paused at the sight of two of Eric's best friends and fellow deputies. They were standing there, not smiling. "Hey, Kayson, Carter . . ." They didn't say anything, it all happened in slow motion. Kayson reached forward, my sleep-addled mind cleared, my knees buckled, and my world crashed down around me.

THE BLACK DRESS that had fit me two weeks ago now hung loose as I took my seat in the front row under the large tent, closest to my husband.

Motorcycles lined the path that wound through the cemetery. Two riders from every force in the state came for the funeral; it was protocol for when another motorcycle deputy fell. I slowly took it all in.

"It's smudged."

Leo, one of my dearest friends, leaned in and whispered, "What's smudged?"

"His casket, look." I pointed to the large, glaring spot. "He always liked things polished." I turned to Kayson, who had stayed close all day just in case I needed anything. "Do you have a handkerchief?"

He pulled a crisp linen square from his breast pocket and handed it over. I got up and moved closer to Eric and began to rub in a circular motion just like I used to do with his shoes. "I know how you always liked things shiny, there, isn't that better? Oh, let me straighten these flowers." I sniffled and tried to clear the tears from my eyes. "I'm sorry that I hadn't decided on a location for our vacation. I'll decide now, come back. I know where I want to go, I do, I promise. I want to go wherever you are. Please." Gentle hands wrapped around me.

"Shhh, I know. Come on." She pulled me back and inched me toward my chair.

I didn't look around to see who all was watching me, watching the pitiful excuse for a woman. I glanced up at my rescuer's eyes. "Stella?" She was another of my closest friends. She and Leo had been pillars of strength for me.

"Yep, I'm right here," Stella answered. Kayson moved down a seat and gave Stella his chair. Leo leaned in, and the two sheltered me as Captain Getty moved to the front and began speaking.

I curled into myself when the bagpipes ruffled the air, and the notes of Amazing Grace rippled deep to my core. I somehow found a way to make myself even smaller when the twenty-one bells rang, each ding echoed on in my ears even after the guard had tolled the last chime. But I slid to the ground, a withered piece of who I once was, my heart bleeding when dispatch called out through Eric's radio.

"Thirteen oh one." I gasped hearing Eric's call numbers. Dispatch repeated, "Thirteen oh one." There was a pause before they continued. "Orange County dispatch, all stations be advised, thirteen oh one has reached his end of watch." I howled in heartbreak, the words piercing me, the future we had planned was over in the blink of an eye. "Show thirteen oh one, ten seven, on January twenty-one, at fourteen hundred forty-six. You patrol the skies, we'll patrol the roads." The radio went off, the color guard moved forward, and then slowly they folded the flag that laid across Eric's casket.

I sat, trying to prepare myself but I couldn't. Nothing could prepare me as I stared at that box that held a shell of the man I had given my heart to, a heart that would never be whole again.

His empty motorcycle riding boots sat next to the coffin, along with his hat, and badge.

The sheriff handed me the flag. "I'm sorry for your loss, Mrs. Haines. Eric was a great deputy," the sheriff said and then moved on.

Eric's boots were placed by my feet, as the assistant deputy sheriff shook my hand. "I'm sorry for your loss." He moved on, and the procession of condolences began.

I was there, giving typical platitudes: *thank you, that means so much, Eric thought the world of you too.* One after another, I spoke them as if they were a five-second song on perpetual replay.

The loud roar of motorcycles as they revved broke through the haze in my mind, and I glanced over and admired the beauty of their formation as, two by two, they drove off.

Slowly the people thinned out, and I figured that before too long, I was going to be alone. But to my utter surprise I was wrong. That night, my friends—my true friends—Stella and Leo were with me. Stella was curled up to my back, Leo at my front, the two of them wrapped me in a net of safety as we slept, and they said nothing during the times I woke and cried.

VIVIAN

J was in the final stretch, or as normal people called it, the reception. I estimated that in about thirty minutes I could sneak out and no one would be any the wiser. It wasn't exactly as if I accepted the request to be part of their bridal party without reservation. Oh hell no, I asked the whole twenty questions, trying to get out of it. Did she have a sister? A cousin? How about her future husband, he have a sister? What about her second grade best friend? Anyone except me. I would have thought someone would catch on, word would spread that I was a horrid bridal attendant, and they would stop asking me, but no. I was a thirty-fucking-two-year-old widow. That alone should have stopped them. Obviously, since I was still being asked, no one cared.

My day sucked, and my night was slowly swirling down the drain. This wedding had me popping Tums and Stella texting me nonstop throughout the day. She was dying to know when the bomb would be dropped.

Some people never grew up; they settle into their comfort zone, whether it is cheerleader attitude in high school or like now, the bride with her eternal, sorority-sisters-for-life mentality. I didn't understand it. Sure, we partied together and shared a sorority house, but when college was over and we went our separate ways that was the end.

This whole wedding had been a clusterfuck; two ladies I spoke to via Facebook and hadn't seen since our ten-year reunion, were in some made-for-television-drama shit. They were best friends and best enemies, always trying to steal the other's thunder—but all innocence, of course.

I glanced at my phone and smiled at the text that had come in.

STELLA: Any bloodshed yet?

Me: No. No one would dare, it doesn't match the color scheme.

Stella: You sorority bitches are too much for me.

Me: Bite me. We aren't all catty.

Stella: Meow. So, has bitch 1 gotten even yet with bitch 2?

BITCH ONE WAS a bride last year when Bitch Two, the maid of honor, announced during her speech that they could share the date forever because she just got engaged, and then shows off the ring. Needless to say, she got applause and sort of stole the bride's thunder. But the shocking part was that Bitch Two was stupid enough to ask Bitch One to be one of her bridesmaids.

ME: Not yet but some strange shit has happened.

Stella: Tell me.

Me: During the ceremony the flower girl dropped blue rose petals instead of ivory. No one knew who did it or took ownership of the mess up. Hell, even the speeches went off without a hitch. I give it to Bitch One, she is standing tall. Shit, gotta go.

BITCH ONE HELD a microphone as if she were going to eat it. I wondered, for the hundredth time, what I was doing there. I should be with Stella and the rest of the gang. Of all of my friends, they were the ones who stood by me while I fell to pieces after my husband was killed. Not to mention we all rode motorcycles, and we all got into some serious shit together. My true friends weren't these ladies. Nope, my true friends were my gang and my sister-in-law, she and I were close and always would be, probably because we had gone through the dark together and survived. She and I had become friends in highschool, and she introduced me to her twin brother.

I tried to tune out Bitch One as she continued in her high-pitched voice, but I couldn't. "We've put together a little surprise for the lovely couple," she announced. Everyone in the audience cooed, but the bridesmaids who had also been in her wedding groaned. We were worried, and her words didn't sound promising. Music started playing, a screen rolled down, images of the bride and groom flashed across as the song, "A Thousand Years" rang out. Okay, I had to admit, it was sweet. There were photos of each of them growing up and then more of them in middle school, high school, college, and as adults. But it was the last photo that truly baffled me . . . an ultrasound.

Bitch One put the mic back up to her mouth. "You might not understand why there were blue petals tossed today. Well, like you said at my wedding, when you announced your engagement during the maid of honor speech, we have something to celebrate together."

"Oh shit," I whispered.

"I'm pregnant, and we just found out it's a boy. Surprise!"

The clapping was a slow roll, but I was done with this bullshit. I tossed my napkin down and headed for the door; I was so outta there. I was done with these petty-ass bitches.

As I walked by the bar that was nestled right by the doorway, I stopped and grabbed an open bottle of champagne. I needed it after this major clusterfuck. Before I took another step toward the door, I leaned back in and grabbed a second bottle just to be safe, then strolled for the elevator as I took a long swig off the first bottle. The bubbles tingled my nose, but the cool alcohol was as refreshing as it was welcome. I was sweating like a whore in church, with all of these damn ruffles.

Pressing *seven*, I tried to drink the entire time the elevator climbed. When the doors opened, I stomped to my room pissed beyond all belief. How dare these women use their weddings, a day to celebrate love, as a battlefield? I loved being married, and I was a good wife. God, I missed waking up next to him.

I locked my door and kicked off my shoes—one going left and the other going I have no idea where. Then I started to wiggle out of my dress. There was no way in hell I wanted to put one of these bottles down, so I did some fancy moves, like the shoulder drop, the twist, and even the pony, the only thing missing was music.

When I was finally free of the taffeta monstrosity, I did my best rendition of Tom Cruise in *Risky Business*, using my pantyhose-clad feet to give me a slide across the not-one-bit-shaggy, nylon-carpeted floor. I used the bottle as my mic and sang about some *Old Time Rock 'N Roll*. I kept singing and practicing my slide until I had finished the first bottle. I swayed a little before I tossed it to the floor, and then a brilliant-beyond-brilliant idea hit me: I needed to call Erin.

Ohh, I missed Erin so much. She was Eric's twin sister, and since he'd died Erin and I still talked about everything, and I mean everything, just not as often as we used to. I was going to call her.

"Stay right there, don't move," I said to the second bottle of champagne as I set it on the nightstand.

"Phone, oh phone, where did I put you?" I called.

I wondered if I could yodel. "Phone-o-ne-o." Nailed it.

There it was, I found you, you little fucker. I snagged my phone from the pocket of my dress and then turned back to the bed. Oh, head spinning. Carefully, I crawled onto the bed, grabbed the bottle of champagne that had been sitting all alone, and took a sip before scrolling through my phone for Erin's number.

AARON

*R*olling forward on the balls of my feet, I lifted my arms and shot. The floor went quiet for the second it took for the ball to zoom through the air and swish through the hoop.

"All net," my coach shouted.

Sweat beaded down my face, the salty tang as it coated my lips was a familiar taste.

"Great practice team, let's end here. Get showered, the bus is waiting out back. See you at ten tomorrow." Coach strode off the practice court. Lenny, one of the team hands, raced around gathering the balls while the rest of the team and I headed off to the showers.

Practice today had been relatively easy; coach didn't want to run the risk of one of his starting players being injured and having to sit this game out.

"God, I need to get laid," Dominic announced. He was a small forward, and it didn't surprise me that this was always the first thing out of his mouth. "Yo, Aaron, you gonna meet us in the bar?"

"No alcohol before the game Dominic. You know the rules," Coach shouted.

"Maybe. My shoulders are killing me." I reached back and massaged the knot before stepping out of the shower and grabbing a towel. I hated when we had away games; every locker room was set up differently, every arena had a different vibe. I headed to the locker that I had claimed earlier and slipped back into my suit. The only part that I was permitted to forgo since we were going straight to the hotel was my tie, but we couldn't have more than two buttons unfastened, and we still had to wear an undershirt. It was the little details like this that made what should be a ten-page contract sixty pages.

Shoving my workout clothes into a laundry bag with my name on it, I dropped it into the cart along with my towel as I left.

Security guards who looked like NFL linebackers lined the way for me out of the host arena. I pushed open the back door to the parking lot and was immediately assaulted by shouting women.

"Aaron, over here."

"I love you, Aaron Skkye."

"Aaron. Aaron."

Holding up one hand to give them a wave, I stayed far away and made my way to the bus. Dominic and a few others hopped out of line to sign autographs and bask in the attention, trying to see if any of the groupies were worth elevating.

What people didn't realize was that just like ball players, people who referred to themselves as *ball bunnies* and *jersey chasers* had their own first string, second string, and bench-warmers. We always saw them hanging around in our hotel lobby. All it would take was me whipping it out and a ball bunny would be on her knees sucking me off.

I took the first seat available as the rest of the team climbed aboard. Once the driver closed the door, Maggie, our team secretary, a middle-aged woman with fire engine red hair, stood up.

"Listen up," Maggie announced. "We are on floor eleven and there will be guards at all stairway exits. If you listed your family as attending, then they have already received a copy of the key. Bus leaves tomorrow morning at ten, don't miss it. Should you miss our departure, you will have to explain why to Miss Romero." Maggie said the same thing every time we got on a bus: she reminded us of some details and then gave the same warning and included the same consequences.

Carmen Romero was the owner of the Lightning, and she was a ball-breaker. None of us wanted to be in her crosshairs.

The bus pulled in front of the Conrad, and Maggie stepped down. As we got off the bus, she handed us our room keys. Our luggage was already in our rooms.

"Aaron, come on man, come hang with us," Hakeem said as he walked down the steps of the bus behind me.

"Nah." I lowered my voice to a whisper. "I've got a bottle of scotch calling my name up in the room."

Ignoring the next throng of women shouting, I grabbed my key and headed for the elevator. When I stepped off, I nodded to the security guard, then went to find my room.

The room itself was about as standard as they got with a full bathroom, minibar, and bed. Hell, at least I had a decent view of the skyline.

I stripped from my suit and tugged on a pair of shorts and a T-shirt before cracking the seal on my bottle of Macallan 24 sitting in my suitcase.

My phone rang, but it wasn't a number I was familiar with, so I ignored it. Grabbing the remote, I scrolled through the channels until I landed on ESPN, but I had to pause when my phone rang again from the same number.

"Hello?"

"Erin, where's Erin?"

"Um, this is Aaron."

The woman, who was obviously drunk, laughed as if I had just said the funniest thing ever. "Really, stop teasing. Get Erin for me."

"This is Aaron, who is this?"

"Erin? Whoa, you sick?"

"No. Why?"

"Your voice, it doesn't sound like you, it's so deep. Head rush."

I chuckled. "Who are you?"

"Erin, don't be stupid, it's me, Vivian."

Deciding to just play along, I smiled. "Hey, Vivian, how are you?"

"Not good. I'm so fucking lonely. I know, I know, you always tell me that it's time for me to move on. Ugh. Do you know how long it's been since I had sex? Can your cherry grow back?"

I coughed, and some highly prized Macallan 24 spewed from my mouth. "I don't think cherries grow back."

"Damn it." Vivian sighed.

"As far as your sex life, I have no clue how long it's been."

"It's been since Eric." Vivian started crying.

Okay, I didn't do crying females, maybe because all my life it had been just my addict mom and me. I was the one who had an excuse to cry, we would be on the move for days at a time with little food and even less money. But it would be Mom crying in fits between her highs.

Vivian was still crying about how much she missed Eric, and I sort of felt sorry for her. I had never been in love, but I could guess that breakups were hard for both sides. "Why, Erin, why? Why did he have to leave me?"

"I don't know, sometimes we all just need to move on, you know, try something different."

"Need to move on? He didn't *need to move on*. We were planning a trip for our five-year anniversary." She panted. "What are you saying? You think Eric wanted to leave me? How could you? I loved him, and I know that he loved me."

Vivian was on a nonstop flow of talk, so I used my time to refill my glass. This poor woman, whoever she was, just needed to vent.

"It's all that . . . that . . . asshole's fault," Vivian shouted.

Oh, there was another woman. "Why did you call me?" I asked.

"What? You don't want me in your life anymore?" Vivian hiccupped. "I need you, Erin."

Her tone was broken enough to squeeze a bit of sympathy out of me. I'd never been needed. Well, except for by my mother when she needed me to bail her ass out of jail, or when she claimed to need food when all she wanted was money for drugs. Still, I wasn't whomever this chick meant to call, so I knew her need wasn't directed at me.

Vivian's words became muffled, and I heard the faint sound of shuffling and things being knocked over. "Vivian, you there? You okay?"

"Yeah, hold your panties . . . santies . . . aunties . . . um, what rhymes with panties?"

Chuckling, I tried to rack my brain, but I couldn't think of anything either. "Not sure."

"Noooot a poet, I know it." Vivian drawled her words out. "That's okay, I grabbed the mini wines from the fridge."

Mini wines? "Where are you?"

"I'm at the hotel, silly, remember? I had that wedding to

go to that you bailed on. Oh my god. Crazy. Why are people like that?"

I didn't want to ask whose wedding she was talking about, and since I had an early flight to catch, I figured my questions would just keep her talking longer.

"They don't get it. But you do, I know you do. He was your brother, but he was my husband." Vivian cried for a few seconds and then went silent.

Was? Oh shit. Exactly how close were she and her brother-in-law?

"Viv, I'm sorry that the wedding upset you."

"Yeah, I . . . I just hate to see . . ." She sniffled. "People make a mockery out of marriage. Eric is never coming back to me. It's been four years, and it still hurts. No one wants to get that call, no one. Eric was their lieutenant, and they had to be the ones to give me the news. Oh god, what am I going to do?" Her words were fading more and more as time went on.

I grabbed my iPad and did a search. I only knew a few things: he was a lieutenant, he passed away four years ago, and was survived by his wife, Vivian. Since her area code was four-oh-seven, I started with Orlando and then entered the rest of the information I knew. It didn't take long before the search engine brought up story after news story.

"Sergeant Haines, posthumously promoted to lieutenant."

"Erskine Sello found guilty on six charges of second-degree murder and two counts of third-degree murder for the death of his girlfriend, their daughter, and six Orange County deputies."

The *Orlando Journal* quoted Vivian as saying, "My

husband was a good man; he always did what was right. He never hurt anyone. And this is what he gets?"

I REMEMBERED WHEN THIS HAPPENED, I had just been drafted, and it was all over the news. Since our home stadium was within walking distance of the Orange County courthouse and sheriff's office, we had front row seats to the protests and news coverage.

"I'll never find love again. I had my one chance . . ." And then Vivian fell silent again, only this time, her words were followed by a soft whistle of air that sounded like snoring. "Good night, sweet, get some rest. Things will get better, I promise." I disconnected and then crawled into my own bed thinking of the sad woman who'd called my number by mistake.

VIVIAN

*T*he ringing, oh my god, the ringing in my head wouldn't stop. I grabbed the extra pillow and threw it over my head, tucking it tight to try to escape the sound. Holy shit, it had been so long since I had a hangover. Headaches, I remember. Cringing at bright lights and loud noises, sure. But ringing? Never.

I sighed when it stopped, but then cringed when it started up again.

Fuck. I tossed the pillow to the ground and searched for my phone. I was sort of shocked that it was nestled against my face and I hadn't realized it. Pulling it away from me, I closed one eye and tried to focus on who was calling . . . Stella.

"Whattt?"

"Wow, you sound like death ran over."

"Thanks, I feel like someone stuffed me like a pillow and all this cotton is coming out of my mouth."

"Well, I'm your morning wakeup call. Don't forget we are all meeting for lunch. So, get your ass up, I'll be there in thirty to get you." Stella was always so bossy.

"But . . ."

"No buts, I told you yesterday when I dropped you off for that calamity of a wedding that I'd pick you up. I'm heading over now. Get ready. You don't want me to pull your ass out of bed."

"I'd like to see you try." I regretted the words once I had said them.

"Bwahaha," Stella cackled. "Challenge accepted." She hung up, and I rolled from bed determined to be ready when she arrived; that woman was crazy-ass scary.

I stumbled into the large shower with faux gold knobs, shower head, and frosted glass. It reminded me of when Eric used to sneak into the shower behind me. I would pretend not to know he was there, but even when my head was under the rushing water and my eyes were closed, there was no missing the sudden cold swish of air that blew in when the shower door was opened. I sighed at the memory of the way he would press my hands against the cool tile and take me from behind.

The memory made me smile.

I was still smiling as I dried off and got dressed. I had just zipped up my suitcase when the phone rang, not my cell but the hotel room.

"Hello?" I was sort of confused why anyone would call me here.

"Miss Haines, this is Mr. Whiteside the hotel manager, we need you to come down to the front lobby."

"Okay, is everything okay?"

Before he could say anything, I heard the problem. "You tell her to get down here right now. This isn't over, no way. She's mine, damn it, mine. Vivian, I love you, love you long time. Remember, remember Long Duck Dong?"

I shook my head; Stella was quoting *Sixteen Candles*. "I'm

sorry, I'll be right down. Tell her that we'll get her meds and not to worry."

"I'll let you tell her. But please hurry, she is quoting Shakespeare to the large rhododendron in the center of our lobby."

I couldn't hold back my laugh as I hung up the phone, grabbed my bags, dropped the keycard on the nightstand, and left the room.

When the elevator doors opened at the lobby level, Stella was standing there twirling her hair and looking as if she were talking to a chair. Security officers were speaking to her, and people were standing around watching the town freak, but she didn't so much as glance their way. "Oh, there you are," Stella shouted and ran to me in her favorite Phoebe-Buffay way, with knees close and heels kicking out.

I held up one hand trying to ward off impact. "Calm down, Stella. We will refill your meds and get you back to the home. Don't worry."

She ground to a halt, looked at me with wide eyes, and then started laughing. "Well played, bitch, well played. Can we go now?"

I took a step toward the front desk and the four clerks in their navy blue suits and ties. They stood in shock until one —I assumed he was the manager because he looked a bit more pompous—realized that I was going to leave Stella unattended.

"You're all set, Miss Haines, we have you all checked out. Your receipt has been sent to your email address on file. Take care of your friend."

I couldn't look the man in the eyes. If I did, I would probably lose it. "Thank you." I wasn't shocked that no one said they hoped to see me soon. Really, who would want me to come back with friends like this? The woman had no shame in her game.

Before we stepped into the revolving door, Stella thrust a pair of sunglasses toward me. "You'll need these. I have water and Excedrin in the car."

"You are forgiven." I slid the glasses up my nose to shield my light-sensitive eyes.

Stella loudly, obnoxiously said what everyone else was thinking but was scared to say, but she was the sweetest, kindest person at the same time. She let me sleep the entire way to Rocco's Tacos.

"Wake up, sleepy head," Stella sing-songed.

I groaned as I uncurled myself from the seat and got out. For some dumbass reason, the sun seemed to be shinning brighter than it had been a few minutes ago. "Who all is meeting us?"

"Everyone probably." Stella flicked her wrist as if it were no big deal, but more people meant more noise, and that was definitely a big deal . . . a huge, ginormous fucking deal.

We walked into Rocco's and I cringed, the sound shooting nails through my head. It took a moment for me to acclimate before I pasted on a smile and waved to a couple of guys I knew from Sixes, the bar that I owned. We wound around a large bar area and headed straight for the back. If the weather was nice, we loved sitting outside. Rocco's had a great area with big, plush, deep furniture that you could really relax into as you took in the lake view.

"Wow, please tell me the look you are sporting is because someone rocked your world last night," Harley, a dear friend and deputy, said as I dropped into an empty seat.

"Yep, two in fact." Everyone stopped talking as if I'd pressed mute. I laughed because nothing changed in this group. If anyone even alludes to sex, they turn into bloodhounds. "Their names were Korbel and Brut, we had a blast, only problem was it didn't last very long, which is why I'm like this today."

"Oh, you poor baby," Sophie soothed as she took the seat on my right and Leo took a seat to my left. I offered them the best smile I could, and they patted my shoulders in sympathy. They were great friends.

I loved being around friends who knew me from when Eric and I opened the bar, who were with me when I first learned how to ride a motorcycle, and friends that I had added along the way. We tried to get together once a month, but unfortunately not everyone always could.

"Sooo, tell me just how bad the wedding was." Stella smiled as everyone leaned in to listen just as our waiter approached. He was maybe in his early twenties and was clearly fighting a tough battle against acne.

"I'm Arwin, what can I get you?"

He turned his attention to me first. "I'd like two steak tacos, a mango margarita, and the largest glass of water you have and keep them coming, please." I gave him my cheekiest smile.

As soon as he got all the orders and promised to be back with chips with guac and salsa, everyone turned their attention back to me.

"Sooo, tell us," Stella demanded.

"Do y'all remember when I told you about a girl from my sorority who was the maid of honor at a wedding I went to last year? The one who stood up to give a speech at the reception, told the bride that she was so excited they were best friends, and that the day would always be special to the both of them. Everyone thought she was talking about the bride and groom, but then she announced her engagement and spent the rest of her speech showing off her ring?"

"I would have stabbed her," Leo growled. Leo was a motorcycle mechanic and although soft spoken, she could be a tad scary when it came to catty women.

"We remember." Stella was nodding, since she already

knew some shit had gone down at the wedding last night. She just didn't know what it was.

"But that was like a year ago, right?" Ariel asked. "What's that have to do with yesterday?"

"The wedding I went to yesterday, was that maid of honor's wedding." I paused and everyone nodded to show they were following along. "She asked the former bride to be her matron of honor."

"No shit," Stella cackled. "Not only is the woman heartless, but also she's a dumbass."

"Anyway, all the other bridesmaids who were in the first wedding were waiting, knowing that at any moment, all hell was gonna break loose. When the wedding coordinator ran in saying the flower girl was tossing out blue petals instead of the ivory ones she was supposed to, we all figured the shit was going to hit the fan, but nothing happened. Then when the napkins on the head table were all exchanged for blue ones, we all braced ourselves. Still . . . nothing. When the former bride started speaking, she had a photo montage for the happy couple projected behind her. The last picture was a sonogram image."

"Oh fuck," Stella hissed and then coughed because she'd breathed in a lungful of her margarita.

"Yep, she happily tells her BFF that, once again, they can share another special date because she had just found out she was having a boy. She had turned the wedding into a freaking gender reveal party."

Groans echoed all around me with the occasional, "You've got to be fucking kidding me," or, "With friends like that, who needs enemies?"

Arwin chose that moment to deliver our food, and I stared at his name once again; it tickled something in my brain. "Can I get anything else for you ladies?" he asked.

When we all said we were good, he left and all eyes returned to me.

"What did you do?" Leo asked.

"I grabbed my two dates and headed to my room." I stopped talking when my phone started ringing with Erin's ringtone. "Where's my purse?"

"Right here," Stella said, leaning forward and grabbing my phone from the top of the bag. She answered it and pressed speaker. "Yo, bitch, haven't seen you in fo-ev-ah."

"Excuse me?" A very male voice came over the line.

I snagged the phone from her. "Hello? Who's this?"

He chuckled. "Vivian, I assume, how's the hangover?"

"Huh? It's fine. Who are you, and why are you calling from Erin's number?"

"As I told you last night, my name *is* Aaron, but I don't know your sister-in-law Eh-rin"—he emphasized the pronunciation of the beginning of Erin's name—"I'm Air-on." I glanced up at the group, who were all giggling and wearing shit-eating grins. Great, more people who I will have to kill for witnessing my humiliation. "Truthfully though, I just called to check on you. You were quite a mess last night, I hated hanging up. You were cute in an Isla-Fisher, *Wedding-Crashers* kind of way." Several of the girls busted out laughing. "I'm so sorry, I didn't mean for others to overhear."

"It isn't your fault. It's mine for allowing it to be on speakerphone and theirs for not allowing it to be any other way. Thank you for checking on me, I appreciate it. As you can tell, I'm good, being suffocated . . ." I paused and winked at the girls, so they knew that I was totally joking. "I'm so sorry for drunk dialing and pulling you into the madness. I must have entered my sister-in-law's new number wrong. I'll fix it. Sorry again."

"No worries, it was nice talking to you for four hours. I'll let you go since you're with friends. Have fun, we'll talk soon." He disconnected before I had a chance to say no need.

"Ooohh, what happened?" Ariel leaned in and asked, her Southern accent thick.

"Talk again?" Leo said as she poked me in the arm.

"No clue, don't remember it at all." I opened my contacts in my phone and searched for Erin's name. Then I groaned because I had two numbers listed for her. "Oh shit, whoever that was must have her old Florida number. I never deleted it when she moved to New York." I deleted the old number so I wouldn't make that mistake again.

"Give me that." Stella snatched the phone and typed before handing it back. "I saved Aaron's number in there so you won't forget it as well. Besides, if he has her old number, it means he lives here. You never know when you might need another drunk dial."

"Kill me now, what if I run into this person or he tells people that I'm a nut job?"

"Did you two exchange photos?" Sophie raised one brow and stared at me with her best mom-inquisition look.

"No." I shook my head for emphasis.

"Did you tell him your full name so he could actually tell people that you are a nut job?" she asked.

"I don't think so."

"Then stop with the drama and just enjoy." She shrugged and held her hands out, waiting for me to say she was right, but I wasn't giving anyone that credit. Instead, I kissed her cheek.

AARON

$\mathcal{W}$e were playing the Bulls, and as usual we arrived early for conditioning but first, we had the concrete catwalk. I glanced around at teammates who were busy trying to fix their laces, smooth out their jeans, and make sure their collar was flat. I was too busy thinking about Vivian to bother.

Exiting the bus, bursts of light flashed as reporters squeezed up to the roped off area to get a shot of who was wearing what. These pictures would go into a file to be used whenever they needed to gossip about us.

As we wound our way inside, I headed to the most remote spot I could find in the United Center and pulled out my phone so I could call her.

I waited as it rang and rang, then her voicemail picked up. "This is, Viv, take me off your calling list. No I'm not interested, but if we really are friends, then you may leave me a message."

"Hey, Viv, it's Aaron. I was just calling to say hi. I'll try you again later."

I hung up and headed to the visiting team locker room. As soon as I entered, I was assaulted.

"Aaron, Mike Carpenter with AFN Sports, how do you feel going against Zach LaVine again? Last time, he powered through and made the winning shot."

I smeared on a forced smile. "Thanks for asking, Mike, I feel great. Coach has been working us harder than ever, and I feel that it has really paid off. We're strong as a team." I took one step forward to let him know questions were over.

"Thanks, Aaron," Mike called after me as I rounded the corner to our lockers and changing area.

"Aaron, plans tonight?" Gage, one of my best friends, asked. He was our team's shooting guard and a lot more levelheaded than a lot of the others. "LeeAnn keeps bugging me to get you to come out with us."

"Thanks, but I thought you and LeeAnn were having some romantic shit tonight. Don't worry about me, I'll be heading to my room and catching up on sleep."

"No date night, we have both the kids with us, so if you change your mind, just holler."

"Will do, thanks." I had totally different plans: I wanted to try to call my midnight caller, she was funny. I opened my locker door and pulled out shorts and a shirt from my duffle bag.

THE SCORE WAS sixty-two to sixty-six, and the Bulls were winning. Dominic recovered the rebound, passed it to Gage, who passed to LeShawn, who shot from the three-point line and scored.

Two down with seven seconds on the clock.

It was their ball, but Dominic stole it from their point guard, brought it over half court and then spun right before crossing over and passing it hard toward where I was supposed to be. I was running, breaking free of my guard and reaching the ball with two seconds left on the clock.

The buzzer blared a second after the ball lost contact with my fingertips, and it was as if time froze, no one moved. A trail of sweat ran into my eyes, but I didn't blink, there was no way in hell I'd miss this moment. Then the ball hit the board, bounced back to the rim of the net, and rolled along the edge, teasing me, that motherfucker, as I held my breath watching it. When it wobbled, I inwardly prayed until it rolled over and into the basket.

The team and Lightning fans in the stadium went wild; although, we were silenced out by the overpowering disappointment of the home team fans. I totally understood that, but I was on cloud nine, we had beaten the Bulls.

"Holy shit, Skkye, that was fucking unbelievable," Gage hollered.

"Aaron."

"Aaron."

Reporters vied to push forward and be the one to get my first quote. I finally stopped once my heart and breathing had slowed a fraction.

"Aaron, Sylvia Summers with NBA TV, you looked a little shocked when Dominic threw the ball to you, any comments?"

"I have to give high praise to Dom for that play, I heard the coach shouting for him to pass it to Casimir, so when it came my way instead, I did what I love to do, I caught the ball and shot."

"Any clue as to why Dominic Flanders passed to you instead of Casimir?"

"Why don't you ask him?" I smiled and then moved in an attempt to get closer to the tunnel.

"Aaron, Mike Overbrook with Beckett Basketball, your

contract is coming up for renegotiation, any truth to the rumors that you are looking at the Lakers?"

I paused, totally taken aback. "Sorry, I can't keep up with the rumors, but I assure you that I'm not leaving. My contract still is solid and so is my commitment to the Lightning." He looked like he was going to ask me something else, but I moved swiftly through the crowd until I was at my locker.

~

BY THE TIME I settled into my seat on the plane that would bring us to the next city we were playing in, it was almost eleven. Too late to call, so I sent a text.

ME: Hey, it's Aaron with an A, lol. I wanted to make sure you're still alive. Hopefully you got some aspirin and tons of water into you.

I WAS STUNNED when the tiny speech bubble appeared followed by her reply moments later.

VIVIAN: I wish I were sleeping. I am actually at work.

Me: Still? What kind of work do you do?

Vivian: I own a bar, which is probably the best job ever.

Me: Sounds like a dream job, but if you're the boss, don't you have people to stay late so you don't have to?

Vivian: I usually do, but she called in sick at the last minute, so it's just me.

Me: You don't have security there with you?

Vivian: Nope. There really isn't any need for it because of where I'm located.

Me: What's the name of it?

"GREAT SHOT, AARON," Casimir said as he passed and patted me on the back.

I nodded and returned to my text.

VIVIAN: I doubt you've eaten here or heard of it.

Me: And why would you say that?

Vivian: My place isn't close to the typical hangouts. Since you have my sister-in-law's old number, I'm guessing you haven't been in the area long, so the odds are in my favor that you've never been here.

Me: Is that your sly way of asking me how long I've lived in Orlando?

Vivian: Ha! You caught me.

Me: I've been there about a year and a half. But I just got this number. How about you, you still in Orlando?

Vivian: Yep, grew up not too far from here and have no interest in leaving. I'm wrapping things up here.

Me: Say no more. I'll let you get closed up and get home. Can I call you tomorrow?

A SPEECH BUBBLE appeared but a new text didn't come through. She was either typing the next Great American Novel or was she second-guessing what she wanted to say. My money was on the latter, but I didn't want her to second guess, I wanted her to jump, follow this crazy urge. Then the words appeared.

. . .

Vivian: Okay
    Vivian: But not before ten

I chuckled.

Me: Deal.

∾

The next morning, I watched last night's game reels, but at quarter after ten, I reached for my phone.

She answered with a groggy, "Hello?"

"Shit, did I wake you?" I asked.

"No, I just haven't had my coffee yet. Hold on, I need to add some sugar and then take a long sip." The sound of a metal spoon hitting the sides of ceramic mug was the only sound I heard, then silence followed by, "Okay, now we can talk. Rule number one is never talk to me before coffee."

"I thought that was rule number two; rule number one was never call you before ten."

Vivian chuckled. "Good memory, and who says men can't be taught?"

"I'm keeping notes or I'll forget. Anyway, sorry about interrupting you with your friends the other day, was just calling to check on you. You were really hammered that night."

"Don't worry about it, it gave them fodder. We're always razzing on someone, might as well have been me that day."

"At least it sounded like you were having fun."

"We were. So, what all did you learn about me the other night, was I a leaky faucet?"

My smile got wider. "No, you were fine. But I know that

you were trying to call your former sister-in-law. You hate that she moved away. You never talk anymore since Eric passed. I'm sorry by the way, I know it must be hard."

"You have no idea," Vivian whispered, and I ached for her. I knew loss but in a totally different way. My loss was by choice.

"You told me about the wedding you had just been to."

"See, you actually know quite a bit about me, tell me about you." I could imagine Vivian tucking her dark hair behind one ear. Hell, for all I knew, she could be a blonde or a redhead, but for some reason, neither of those felt right.

"I'm sort of boring. Work consumes a lot of my time."

"What do you do?"

I could just tell her who I was, but I didn't want her to see me as a walking, talking wallet. "I work for Romero Holdings."

"Oh, I've never heard of them."

Not a shocker there.

"They own a lot of businesses."

"Yeah? Like what?"

"Well, they are mainly an investment company, and the owner, Carmen Romero, runs a bunch of large and small franchises. I'm one of many who help keep it all running." A roil in my stomach let me know that I was crossing the line to dishonesty. I was misleading her, and that wasn't fair. But my brain kept saying, give it a little longer.

"How about family? Any siblings?" Vivian's voice softened, as if she were relaxing into the conversation.

"I'm an only child, parents are gone." Well, sort of gone, but that was a story for another time. "How about you, family close?"

"Parents are both gone, but I'm close to my friends." We were both silent for several seconds. "So, if you don't mind, can I ask how old you are?"

"Sure, I'm twenty-four." The sound of Vivian coughing echoed across the line. "Are you okay? Is something wrong with my age?"

"Nope, you're fine. Twenty-four is a great year for you, for scotch, but for me that was eight years ago."

"So? You're thirty-two. I bet you're a sexy thirty-two-year-old."

"Umm, no. I'm a tired, been-through-more-than-anyone-should-have, working nonstop thirty-two-year-old."

"Nah, I'm thinking that I have a hot cougar on the line."

"No. Not quite but close. Hey, we are just talking on the phone after a drunk dial, we might be friends, and that's a big might, but we're still pretty much strangers."

"We can change that, want to FaceTime?" I asked, knowing that was a huge jump that I hadn't really considered the ramifications of. What if she recognized me?

"Absolutely not. I'm not ready for that."

"Okay, calm down, I didn't mean to worry you, it was really more of a joke. Let's spend more time talking and texting, okay?"

"Yeah, okay."

"Vivian?"

"Yes?"

"I'd like to be friends, let's build that first, okay?"

"I'd like that." The sigh of relief that escaped her mouth assured me I had just done the right thing.

VIVIAN

 ay Seven . . .

VIVIAN: Hey

Aaron: Hey to you.

Vivian: Did I catch you at a bad time?

Aaron: It's never a bad time for you to text. How was work? Just get home?

Vivian: Yep, just got home. Work was work, always the same, which is what I like. I'm a creature of habit. I don't know if I told you, I call it a bar but we also serve food so I guess it is more of a grille.

Aaron: What's the name again?

Vivian: Ha ha, haven't told you yet.

DAY TEN . . .

. . .

AARON: Heading to the airport, I'm exhausted. Can't believe we stayed up until three this morning talking.

Vivian: I can't believe it's already noon.

Aaron: Tell me something about yourself that others don't know.

Vivian: Okay, but you will have to do the same.

Aaron: Absolutely.

Vivian: I stole a pack of gum when I was four, and my mother made me take it back inside and apologize. I was so upset because she wouldn't go in with me. I remember turning and glaring at her because she just stayed where she could still see and hear me and refused to give me any moral support.

Aaron: Oh, but I bet you were so cute that the store owner just smiled and let you walk off.

Vivian: I don't remember what the guy at the store said, I was too busy being mad at my mom.

Aaron: LOL

Vivian: Okay, now you.

Aaron: I've never broken a law, not even speeding.

Vivian: WTF? Really? I'm a speed demon. Are you uptight?

Aaron: No, my mother was in and out of jail all of my life and I would get shoved off to foster care. In my mind, I can't mentally let loose enough to risk getting in trouble with the law.

Vivian: Oh, I'm so sorry, but that makes total sense. It's okay, I speed enough for the both of us.

DAY FOURTEEN . . .

VIVIAN: Good morning.

Aaron: Wow, it's before ten.

Vivian: I have a few errands to do before work. Where are you headed today?

Aaron: San Antonio.

Vivian: I was just scrolling up through all of our messages, do you realize we've texted every day since I drunk dialed you?

Aaron: Yeah, and we've also talked every day since then as well.

Vivian: Or night, we usually talk at night.

Aaron: I like our nightly talks. I fall asleep talking with you.

Vivian: Literally, you've fallen asleep several times.

Aaron: Sorry.

Day Twenty-One . . .

AARON: I'm heading back to Orlando a week from Thursday and will be home for a while. What do you say we go out for dinner?

Vivian: Yeah, I think that would be nice. Want to Face-Time first?

Aaron: Yes, but I was afraid to ask.

VIVIAN

My eyes were set on the next table, cleaner in one hand, rag in the other, as I strode for it keeping my head down and making no eye contact with anyone. There was too much going on in my head, and I was an open book. If anyone saw me, they would badger the hell out of me, and I would cave, I always cave.

FaceTime, we were going to talk face-to-face via video chat. He was twenty-four, I was a thirty-two-year-old widow, for Christ's sake. I had been through a lot and it showed. How was I going to cover these eternal bags under my eyes that were so deep and dark, no amount of makeup would hide them?

"She's just going to ignore us."

"Nah, she's just in heavy thought."

"Nope, she is trying to avoid us and the world around her."

"Vivian would never ignore us."

"Bullshit, something is on her mind. We need to beat it out of her."

I burst out laughing and set the rag and cleaner down on

the table, but then had to blink my eyes a few times to clear the grittiness of exhaustion. God, I hadn't had a deep sleep in just over four years. I pasted on a smile and turned, mustering up my best Robert De Niro impersonation. "You talking to me?"

It wasn't all that great.

"As a matter of fact, they were," Leo said as she pointed over to Sophie and Stella. "Now spill, what's going on? The two of them have been trying to get your attention, and you didn't even notice."

I glanced over at my manager, Mikki, who seemed to have everything under control and then took a seat at the table.

"It's Aaron," I explained.

"Drunk dial dude?" Leo asked, and I nodded. "You two are still talking?" I nodded again. "What's going on? It's been almost a month, right?"

"Three weeks." I slid my hand across my forehead. "We text every day, talk every night. God, I really like talking to him, and he makes me laugh."

"Then what's the problem?" Leo asked.

"I still feel like there's too much I don't know."

"Um, that's what dating is for. It's the test drive to make sure you want to actually buy it," Stella added in.

"But there are things that he is so vague about."

"Like?" Stella waited for my answer.

"I don't know, I can't think right now. All we're doing right now is taking our time and building a friendship," I explained but left out the fact that anymore, my night felt incomplete if I didn't hear his voice. "Oh, by the way, he's twenty-four."

"So?" Bridget asked. "I'm twenty-four."

"Bridge, I'm thirty-two."

"Ah, cougar." Bridget laughed.

"Who cares?" Leo shrugged and a few others agreed.

"Dude, there is actually a formula to figure out if you are a cougar or not," Stella announced.

"What? Where did you hear this?" Bridget asked.

"I don't remember, but you half the woman's age and then add seven. That's the max age the guy can be to make the woman a cougar."

"I have no clue where you come up with this shit," Leo added.

"She's right, I've read that too somewhere. In all truthfulness, my age has never bothered me before, but then again I wasn't comparing myself to a twenty-four-year-old." Truthfully, thirty-two wasn't old. My biggest fear was that Aaron and I would have nothing in common. He was probably still into partying and hooking up with random women; I was into a glass of wine and Netflix for an episode of *Breaking Bad*.

"Look, we've lost her," Leo whispered.

"She's a goner. He must have some magical phone powers," Stella added.

"Really? I can totally hear you all. No, I just have a lot on my mind. The whole thing is stupid. I drunk dial someone, and a little over three weeks later we are still talking. I have no clue why." I stood up and began pacing around the table. "He's twenty-four, holy shit, twenty-four. I mean, what kind of person does that make me?" I shoved my hands through my hair as if I could push the answers in there, but no dice. True, I was twenty-three when Eric and I finally got married, but we had been high school sweethearts. "Now he wants to see me, like *see* my face, and I agreed. Do you know how long it's been since I've had a good night's sleep? These dark circles have turned into stains they have been under my eyes that long."

"Are you finished yet?" Leo asked. "This pity party has run its course."

"Yes, I'm finished." I let out a huff.

"What does he do?" Leo asked, trying to soothe the situation.

"Oh, that's it." I snapped my fingers. "He says that he works for Romero Holdings, but I have no idea what he *actually* does there."

"Never heard of it." Stella grabbed her drink.

"Me neither, he said they owned lots of franchises. So really, he could do anything. I don't even know what kind of franchises they own."

Sophie had her phone out while Stella leaned over and read over her shoulder. "Well, fuck a duck, they own the Orlando Lightning."

I stared at her for clarity, because I had no idea that a freaking basketball team was a franchise. I thought only fast food places and hotels were franchised out.

"The Lightning, as in, our NBA team," Leo clarified, but I was still giving her a blank look. "Woman, I have no clue how you function sometimes." Leo smiled letting me know that she was totally teasing.

"I knew that," I huffed.

"Exactly." Stella jumped out of her seat, her hands waving in the air is if she were flicking water off them. "*Ding, ding, ding,* we have a winner. That is why you need to talk with him. Twenty-four matters only if that is his IQ." Stella grinned.

"Really? You want me to keep talking to him because of a basketball team?"

She nodded.

"Fine, I'll talk with him, but he might not work for them. He said Romero owns several franchises."

"What if he's a basketball player? Twenty-four is the right

age for a player, right? Quick, is there an Aaron on the team?" Stella asked.

"Yeah, only the best shooting guard in the NBA, Aaron Skkye," Mikki said from behind me.

I turned and stared at her.

"What?" Stella asked.

"She's a basketball junkie, she goes to all the games she possibly can," I explained. And with where this conversation was headed, I needed to extricate myself before they were marrying me off to some nonexistent NBA player. "Hey, been great chatting, but I have to get back to work, I still have bookwork to do." I blew kisses to the girls and headed back to my office. I pulled my phone out of my pocket and saw two missed calls.

I turned to the mirror mounted on the back of the door, cringed and then reached for my small makeup bag so I could do a quick touch up. One last pat down of my flyaway strands, followed by a quick dash of lipstick, and I was as ready as I was going to be.

Taking a deep swallow and an even deeper breath, I dialed his number via FaceTime. He answered on the first ring, but I had my hand over the camera and screen.

"Hello, I'm so glad to hear from you. But I can't see anything."

"I'm blocking it, I can't see you either. I didn't want you to pick up and be shocked and have a heart attack or something."

"I'm young, and . . . I don't know, um, virile. I think my heart is safe."

I laughed. "You've been warned, I'm going to remove my hand."

"Please."

I quickly slid my hand off the phone, showing myself at the same time as I saw him.

He was adorable in a hot and sexy kind of way. He brought his other hand up to scratch his jaw, and my breath freaking caught. The man had the kind of hands a woman would want on her.

"Holy fuck." I slapped one hand over my mouth, shocked that I had said that out loud. Then Stella's words came to my mind about a twenty-four-inch dick, and I had to pinch my lips tight because big hands and all that.

Aaron's hearty laugh bellowed through the phone. "Damn girl, I'm so glad you said that. At least I know I'm not the only one with a habit of cussing. I was trying to watch my mouth around you."

"You'll be right at home around my friends."

He seemed to be concentrating on my picture, and in that moment, I was thankful I had fixed myself before the call. "You're beautiful."

"You're not so bad yourself."

"So, FaceTime is okay now?" I nodded. I felt like a preteen, the only thing missing was the bubble gum that I could stretch and twirl while I stared at my shoes playing coy.

"It's weird; I'm not sure what to say. I feel like I know you and at the same time I'm meeting you for the first time.

"I feel like I've known you forever, like we're best friends who haven't seen each other in years. Except for Gage—"

"Your friend from work?"

"Yeah, besides him, you're the only other person I really talk to," Aaron said.

"I think that's the big difference between men and women. Women have more of a gang mentality. We need a tribe around us. I can think of about twelve friends who I see almost weekly that I could call at any time to air something out with. A perfect example is you."

"Oh, I made the list?"

"You did. Though, I might kick some of my other friends off the list. They've been giving me one hell of a hard time because it's been three weeks and we are still talking. I mentioned you worked for Romero Holdings. They said that was the owner of the Orlando Lightning, the basketball team."

"Yep, that is who I work with," Aaron confirmed, as if working with famous people was no big deal. "Look up the Lightning schedule and you will know where I'm always traveling to."

"Aaron, can I ask you something?"

"Anything, but if it's about my job, can it wait until we meet in person?"

"Yeah, of course."

I wish I had just asked him outright, but if he asked me to wait, I would.

"Hey, I have to run. I have a red-eye flight tonight, and my ride leaves in fifteen minutes."

"Oh, okay, be safe."

"It was nice seeing your face, you are so beautiful. I want to see you again."

"I'd like that." I disconnected and then moved the mouse on my computer and typed: "Orlando Lightning Schedule."

I GOT nothing done yesterday after talking to Aaron. If he followed the Orlando Lightning everywhere, it meant he would probably be back in Orlando sometime today.

I got to work on placing the weekly orders, from food to alcohol and finally, supplies. I opened QuickBooks and began entering the latest receipts and balancing the records. I was lost in my routine tasks, and once they were all entered, I moved on to payroll. By the time that was done, it was almost time to do the line check before the dinner rush started.

The chatter of voices from my dining area dimmed, and it took me a second to glance to the security camera feed on my computer to find out why. I studied the crowd, wondering what was going on. Several people were all looking toward the door. When I spotted Mikki, I got nervous because she looked like a kid at a parade and her favorite float was passing. She was jumping up and down with a ridiculous expression on her face. Panning the area, I spied a familiar face, and my heart did a quick double beat. Aaron, FaceTime, drunk dial, Aaron was here, and he had captured several people's attention, especially Mikki's.

Aaron was very businesslike in a suit that was custom made for his body and hugged every inch of him. The man was meant to wear suits that was for sure.

"Vivian, you aren't going to believe who just freaking walked in." Mikki barged into my office. "Aaron friggin' Skkye, that's who. The one I mentioned to you just the other day, the shooting guard—"

I held up my hands to stop her. "I know who Aaron is."

"He won the Maurice Podoloff Trophy, which is given to the league's most valuable player," Mikki mumbled, trying to add something of value that I maybe didn't know, but then she froze, her eyes blinking slowly before going wide. "Whoa, wait a minute, how do you know Aaron?"

"Long story."

AARON

I couldn't believe that I was nervous. I'd lucked out seeing the name Sixes Bar & Grille on a box in the background. When we hung up, I looked it up and was happy to find out it was close to the stadium. After practice, I headed here, knowing that I only had about an hour before I had to be back at the stadium for our eight o'clock game.

I pulled open the heavy wooden door, and the sounds of laughter and people talking assailed me. Since I'd grown up in a small town in Indiana, this was the type of place I was used to going to. It was a place only the locals knew about, where people gathered just to shoot the shit and spend an evening relaxing.

I ducked under the doorframe more out of habit than necessity. When you're six-eight, you learn to duck after the first time you almost knock yourself out.

When I glanced up, almost everyone was staring at me.

"What can I get you?" Danny, according to his name tag, asked.

"Just water. I'm looking for Vivian."

He fixed me a glass with ice and then added the water. "Someone has already gone to get her."

"How did they know I was here for her?"

"She didn't. But since this is mainly"—he pointed his chin to behind me—"a cop and fireman hangout, when the shooting guard for the Orlando Lightning walks in, the owner gets summoned." He smirks and slides me my glass.

"So, I'm assuming the whole idea of flying under the radar is shot, right?"

"Pretty much, but don't worry, these guys are good people. They won't bother you."

I nodded my thanks, and he rapped a knuckle against the bar. "Great game the other night against the Bulls, by the way."

"Thanks."

"Vivian should be out in a second. Let me know if you need anything else, okay?"

"I will. Thanks."

The guy walked away to pour a draft for another customer, and I took a second to mentally shake off the nerves that were trying to crawl their way up my spine.

Fuck. What was I thinking just showing up here like this? I needed to leave. My eyes tracked toward the door as I berated myself for being so stupid. I had just crossed a million and one boundaries and landed in the stalker zone. Leaving a five-dollar bill on the counter as a tip, I pushed back my stool, already having my mind set on slipping out before she even knew I was there.

I was almost to the door when I heard her, "Going somewhere, Aaron?" I turned and met a little thing of a woman with black hair and bright green eyes.

Two men walked up, both were wearing sheriff uniforms, one was very Mediterranean looking. Vivian turned her attention to them. "I love you, both of you. You can go home and tell your wives that this is who Vivian drunk called."

I listened feeling a little more relaxed realizing that they at least knew about our story.

"You got drunk and called an NBA star?" the deputy with blond hair said. "Forget my wife, I think you need to worry more about my sister. Stella is not going to let you live this down."

Vivian turned back to me, "Aaron this is Deputy Carter Lang and Deputy Kayson Christakos." She pointed to each man. "I've known them forever and Carter's sister is one of my closest friends. When the guys got married their wives joined my group of close friends."

I shook hands with each of them.

"Now that you all know each other, excuse us." Vivian tugged my hand and pulled me toward the back of the bar, to what was clearly her office.

"Mikki, good god woman," Vivian snapped. "Will you excuse us please?"

"But . . . but this is Aaron Skkye, he's the reason I try to get all home games off."

"Mikki, please." Vivian met her employee with a no-joking, don't-push-me kind of eye glare. I fought not to chuckle.

As Mikki left the office, she closed the door behind her, and I stepped closer to Vivian. "Sorry to drop in unannounced, but I only have a few minutes before I'm due back at the stadium."

"You're a professional basketball player?"

"I am."

"Then why lie and tell me you work for Romero Holdings?"

"That wasn't a lie that is who I actually work for." I stepped closer and cupped her face. It wasn't the right time, she wasn't ready for me to kiss her, but god, I wanted to. "I was so close, we were so close, and . . . I needed to see you, face-to-face." Vivian patted her hair. "Stop, you look adorable."

"I have no makeup on."

"I don't care." I tilted her head up to face me. "Go out with me."

"Where?"

"Not sure yet but on a date. Please."

She bit her lower lip, and her eyes seemed to have a hard time meeting mine. "Okay. I'm nervous though."

"Why?" My thumb trailed along her cheek.

"It's been about eighteen years since I went on a first date."

"You haven't been on a date since . . ." I didn't want to finish that sentence.

She shook her head.

I leaned forward and kissed her cheek before whispering, "We will make it special." When I pulled back enough to look her in her eyes, I added, "I'll pick you up at six thirty tomorrow night, I'll get your address from you later."

"Okay." The smile she gave me was heart stopping.

"I hate to meet and run, get it, see what I did there? Eat and run." I was chuckling at my own joke, which was lame, so I stopped and took a deep breath. "But, truthfully, I have to go, Little One. Promise to text me your address?"

She nodded, and I fist pumped.

"Your destination is on your right," the female British voice that I had programmed for my GPS said. I slowed down and turned into the driveway of a small bungalow-style home.

Since picking up a basketball, I'd never felt out of place because I always had somewhere I belonged. Sitting in her driveway, though, I was totally lost.

I had no clue where I would fit into her world. I mean, I loved my car. An Aston Martin Vanquish had been my dream car growing up, but here in this neighborhood, it was too flashy, and I knew it.

My head tilted forward, resting against the steering wheel; I regretted tonight's decisions. Making some last minute changes, I tucked the blue wrapped gift into the glove box. I didn't think it was any big deal, a charm bracelet from Tiffany with a champagne bottle, a phone, and a basketball. But she might, and that was all that mattered.

I headed up to her front door with a bouquet of flowers. The path was spotless. There was no dirt or cobwebs—hell, even my house had stray leaves and pine needles on my front walkway. I didn't have to knock before she was opening her bright red door and greeting me.

"I was worried about you for a second," she said in place of hello.

"Why?"

"You stayed in your car for a while."

"Oh, just nervous, don't want to screw this up. Speaking of, these are for you." I thrust the bouquet forward.

"Come on in, let me set these in some water." I followed her through her small house, feeling more and more like Baymax than the physically fit guy I was.

Her home smelled of vanilla, warm and inviting. I stayed at the edge of her kitchen as she moved to a cabinet, placed one hand on a vase, and froze. She stood there for a few seconds, and I couldn't stand it, I moved to her. Wrapping one arm around her and slowly placing my other hand on hers to keep her from dropping the glass vase that obviously had meaning.

"I've got it." I set it on the counter and then wrapped my arms around her tightly, holding her and no longer feeling like some giant catastrophic mess.

Vivian tilted her head and leaned closer to me. For the life of me, I couldn't resist it. I wanted to wait until the end of our night, but now was right. Sliding one hand to the back of her head, I pulled her mouth closer to mine. Our lips touched for the barest of seconds before my tongue was diving in, splashing into a world of tastes, the mint of toothpaste, her sweetness that seemed to permeate every inch of her body, and something fruity that matched the scent of her shampoo. Our tongues twirled, before I pulled back and then dove back in, almost to the same beat that I desperately wanted to move our bodies to.

Vivian moved her hips closer to mine; she was pressed against my erection. She was reacting in the heat of the moment, but I didn't want any regrets between us, I wanted so much more.

"Come on, Little One, we better get going or we will miss our reservation."

"Oh, sorry, did I cause us to run late?" Her face squinted.

"It was totally your fault, or rather your mouth's, it was too damn delectable to pass up. Let's get your flowers in water and get on the road."

It only took three minutes, then we were in the car, and we were walking into the restaurant only a minute or two past our reservation time.

"Mr. Skkye, we're so glad you're here, we have your table ready just as you requested. Please follow me."

I lowered my head to whisper to Vivian, "Have you ever seen *Young Frankenstein?*"

"The movie? Hell yes." She threw one hand over her mouth, and we both laughed as I tugged her closer

"Yeah the movie. You know when Igor says, 'Walk this

way,' and everyone hunches over and walks like him. I've always wanted to do that. Like walk like her. Look, she has one hand on her hip. It would be so funny." I stopped talking when we reached our table in the back corner of the restaurant. I had requested a four-top table with two chairs both facing away from the rest of the patrons.

A server stepped up to pull Vivian's chair out for her, but I moved into his way and helped her myself.

Once I was seated as well, we accepted our menus, the server opening them to make sure we received the correct ones. Chatham Place was one of the, if not the most expensive restaurant in Orlando, but the food was worth it. There were two different menus, one for the date and one for the bill payer. The difference was that only the bill payer's had prices next to items.

"It seems you know your way around the place, is this where you bring all of your dates?" Vivian asked.

"Believe it or not, I don't date a lot, and no, I've never brought a woman here. The team actually reserves the whole place for meetings, so we can eat while being lectured." In my peripheral, I saw someone coming toward us. "Quick, give me your phone."

"Why?"

I laid my hand on the table open, palm up. "Gimme, hurry."

Vivian quickly grabbed her purse, but it was too late.

"Sir, Madam, I have a chilled bottle of Armand de Brignac Ace of Spades," the sommelier said as he showed me the label and waited for me to approve the bottle. I nodded, and he popped the cork.

"Is that champagne?" Vivian asked. I just smiled. "Smart ass."

"I thought it was funny." Once we received our glasses,

the bottle was wrapped with a cloth and set into an ice bucket on the edge of the table.

"To a great night." I held up my glass.

"And continuing to learn more about each other." Vivian brought her glass up to mine, and they *tinged*. "So, what was up with the camera?"

I took another sip and then set my glass down. "I saw someone walking toward us, and his eyes were focused on me. All I could think of on the fly was for us to get all cozy and take couple photos. But the waiter came with the champagne and the man turned away."

"Does that happen a lot?"

"Me asking for strange objects and then a waiter appears?" Vivian raised one brow. "Oh, you meant interruptions."

"Yeah."

"More than I'd like but not nearly as often as someone like Michael Jordan or Shaquille O'Neill."

Our food was quickly delivered, and the night seemed to be blowing by; I had no clue how to slow it down.

"I'm really shocked you know *Young Frankenstein*," Vivian deadpanned.

"Why?"

"It was kind of before your time."

"Bullshit," I hissed. "That movie came out like fifty years ago, so it was before your time too."

She cracked up, and I sat there admiring the way her eyes lifted the same time the corners of her mouth did, and how her laugh wasn't soft or loud, it was just contagious. I could listen to her laugh for hours. I glanced around and saw other diners watching her as well, and they too were smiling at Vivian.

"Hey, come to my game tomorrow night."

"Uh, what?"

"I have a home game tomorrow night, come as my guest, please. You can bring a friend or two, whatever. I just want you to be there."

"Are you sure? You won't be embarrassed having this older woman sitting there?"

"Okay enough with the older woman shit, no more, I mean it. Find something else to pick on me about because eight years is not that big of a gap. I want you there. Please, Little One."

"Let me see what I can do. Mikki tries to take off as many home games as she can. Let me see what she has planned."

"Just text me and let me know if you can make it and if you're going to bring anyone with you. I'll leave passes for you and them at will call."

"*I* have no fucking clue what I'm going to do." I plopped down in a chair at the table where several of my friends had dropped in for lunch and to be nosy about last night's date.

"Was it that bad?" Sophie asked with a mouth full of salad. "Carter couldn't stop laughing about how you drunk dialed an NBA all-star."

"No, it was wonderful. He's wonderful, really, really wonderful. He scares me because he makes me feel things, but he's so damned understanding when I have momentary breakdowns. He just holds me and lets me cry."

"Sounds sorta perfect to me," Leo said. "Sometimes, that's what we need, someone who sees what we need even when we don't."

"Sounds like you're talking from experience there," Kat said and then directed all of her attention on Leo.

"Touché." Leo smiled brightly.

"All of this is nice, but it isn't my problem. My problem is that I'm going to piss Mikki off, and I never want to do that." I slammed my hands flat on the table.

"Why?" Stella asked.

"Aaron invited me to a game . . . tonight."

"She's going to kill you." Sophie half laughed, half sighed with sympathy. "I mean that, she's already hiding her jealousy over you dating her dream man." This had us all chuckling.

"Exactly, and now I need to see if she will work tonight so I can go watch him play. Oh, I can take a friend or two. But, I've decided I'm going to text him and tell him that I can't come."

"Don't, ask her if she can work and explain it to her, she will understand. She wants to see you happy. She's been with you since the day this place opened." Leo rubbed my back.

I WAS in jeans and a gray T-shirt because it was the closest that I had to the Lightning colors of blue and silver. Mikki, on the other hand, had #33 painted on one cheek and was wearing a jersey with the name Skkye above the number thirty-three on the back, silver tennis shoes with blue shoelaces, and jeans with basketballs embroidered all over them.

"What are you doing dressed like that?" I asked.

"I'm going to put the game on the television and cheer from here."

"I'm sorry Mikki, if this is too much, you go."

"Nope, you both go." I turned to face the door as Leo, Sophie, Ariel, and several others walked in.

"Oh fuck no, there is no way I'm going with her," Stella announced as she walked into Sixes wearing jeans and an Orlando Lightning shirt. "Jeans and jersey are fine, rest of the shit goes."

"Stella, I brought you some decals for your face and

brought you some blue and silver basketball beads. Oh and glasses, see?" Mikki pulled items out of her bag.

"Oh, well then, you can stay. Give me that shit. Let's go all freak."

"Whoa, wait a minute, what's going on?" I practically shouted.

"I've worked restaurants most of my life," Kat, a motor-cycle deputy and one of our close friends, said as she walked into the bar. "Hell, I still do when my parents are desperate for help in theirs. I'm stepping in to help."

"I called Alexis, and she should be here in a few to help as well," Mikki added. Alexis was one of my full-time wait-resses, but she usually worked days.

"But I told him that I was coming alone, he won't have passes for all of us." I suddenly was worried.

"Yes he will," Stella said, her head bobbing with stupid sunglasses. "I still had Erin's old number, so I called him and told him what we had planned. He's got us covered."

"Thank you." I kissed one finger and held it up and waved it. I caught myself, that was something I used to do with—. No, I'm not going there, not now.

"Have fun!" was yelled out. "Can't wait to hear what all happens." I wasn't sure who had said that, so many people had gathered around. "Make her be wild." Was the last call I heard before I was outside and heading to Stella's Tahoe.

"I have instructions." I pulled out my phone and read the text out loud. "We are to find the lot marked blue lot, city officials only and give Aaron's name. They will need my ID."

We were only about five minutes away and with traffic, so the hardest part was finding the blue lot. When we finally did, I realized why: it was only for about twenty cars.

Stella pulled up so the guard was more on my side; he reminded me of John Candy. "This is a reserved lot."

"Thank goodness. I believe there is a spot reserved for me. My name is Vivian Haines, Aaron—"

"Of course Ms. Haines, park anywhere. Walk right through here and you can use the back side of will call. There is never a line; it is for VIPs."

"Thank you so much." I rolled up the window and turned to Mikki, who was sitting in the back.

"Thank you, thank you so damn much for bringing me. I still hate you for encroaching on Aaron, but if you keep up these perks, I might learn to forgive you. Can you ask him who else is single?"

"You're weird." I shook my head.

"Okay ladies, let's go check out this man of Vivian's and maybe find an extra for Mikki."

We headed in the direction the guard had pointed, stopping to clear thorough security before stepping up to what looked like a teller window. "Hey, whose tickets do you need?" a woman asked without turning to face us. She was busy working with the fan in front of her, he was still outside.

"Aaron Skkye, there should be three tickets," I answered.

Without skipping a beat, she reached into her drawer, grabbed an envelope, scanned the three of us, and turned her focus back at me. She opened the envelope and studied the passes. "What's your name?"

"Vivian Haines, this is Stella—"

"Good enough, here you go." She slid me the envelope and went back to helping the fan at the other window.

I pulled out the lanyards and handed them out. "Oh. My. God. He gave us Lightning passes." Mikki kissed the plastic card and then prayed to the Almighty above.

"I figured since that's the name of his team."

"No, there are three levels of tickets: silver, blue, and lightning. Most of the people who come in here are silver.

They have their seats. Blue has special seating, maybe even a box, plus they get extras like if there is a before game or a meet-the-team thing after a game. It's never the whole team, just a player or two. Last but not least, there are lightning passes: spouses have those, maybe parents, but that is about it. You can go into the tunnel. You will have someone come check on you and your comfort. It is the best of the fucking best."

"Is that all, Mikki?" I fought to hold back my grin.

"Is that all? You're kidding me, right?"

"Yes, I'm kidding you. We're here to show support. Who wants to get a drink and snack?" I asked and moved toward a concession stand.

Mikki grabbed my arm. "Don't, I'm serious. Food is brought to us. Trust me, please."

"I say we trust her. Look at her. She matches most of these people, you look like the freak." Stella pointed to me. "Not so sure we should be seen with you." Stella wrapped an arm around me. "Maybe we'll forgive you this time. Come on." Her beads jangled.

"Are you going to take those sunglasses off?" I asked.

"Nope, I make this shit look good." She placed a finger at the tip of one arm of the glasses and wiggled them. Do I look like Rizzo from *Grease?*"

"More like Jan." I waited for her comeback.

Without missing a beat, she lifted one leg behind me, brought it up, and kicked my butt.

"Where are our seats?" I asked Mikki.

"They're in the first row—holy shit, we have seats behind the bench."

"I'm totally lost," I said to Stella.

"Me too."

We followed Mikki down stair after stair, a mixture of leather, plastic, and sweat sort of filled the air. It was not overwhelming, but it was there. I wondered how someone got rid of the smell of sweat, or if it was like old bars with the smell of smoke, there was nothing you could do, it was in the very fibers of the foundation.

Our seats were directly behind a bench. "That's where our players sit," Mikki announced. "You'll get to see Aaron up close and personal."

I smiled when I spotted the souvenirs that had been left for us, and my smile only got bigger when I took in what was in my seat.

"Put it on." Mikki grabbed the jersey from the stack and slid it over my head. "It's his official jersey."

"It's so big." I held it away from my body. "It's practically a dress."

"Yeah, because it is really his. Like one of his that he *wears*. I'm so jealous."

I picked up the tote bag that was full of socks, decals, beads, clackers, and all the other swag that Mikki seemed to come with. But it was the pale blue envelope that caught my attention.

Sliding one nail under the flap, I opened it and slid out the card. A simple matching blue correspondence card.

VIVIAN,

I'm glad you came tonight. Let me take you home. After the game, I have to go to the locker room, but I'll hurry. I'll meet you at our tunnel.

Aaron

"WHICH IS THE LIGHTNING'S TUNNEL?" I asked Mikki.

"That one"—she pointed to her left—"and the one on the right is for the visiting team. They lead to the locker rooms."

"I don't care about tunnels, what did the letter say?" Stella asked. I handed it over before flagging down someone.

"May I get you something?" a woman in what could only be described as caterer clothes asked.

"Can we just get some sodas?"

"Absolutely." She called off the list of drinks. "Coke, Diet Coke, Sprite, Mr. Pibb—"

"Diet Coke," we all said in unison.

"May I grab you something from the salabars or would you like something else?" She waited for our answers.

"If it isn't too much trouble, can I have a hotdog?" The food over there looked fancy, come on, they had carving boards—oh, excuse me, salabars—but I just wanted something simple.

"No trouble at all. A lot of people still want their stadium dogs, kind of a staple. Anyone else?"

"Me, hotdog," Stella agreed.

"Me too, mustard only," Mikki added.

"I'll bring you all sorts of condiments." She left, and I turned to Stella, who had handed the note over to Mikki.

"He really likes you." Stella placed one hand on top of mine.

"You can tell that from this letter?" I asked, taking the letter back and tucking it into the tote.

"Yeah. He seemed genuine about wanting to spend time with you. It was sweet."

"You got that from four sentences?"

"Positive affirmation, I tell you, he was going for positive affirmations." Stella locked eyes with Mikki. "Don't you agree?"

"Yep. He didn't give you fan stuff; he gave you his real jersey. The expensive signed stuff is on jersey replicas. Oh shit, I didn't look. Turn around." Mikki grabbed hold of my shoulders and twisted me.

"What are you doing?"

"Awwee, here it is. He wrote, '*My Vivian,*' and signed it."

Stella pulled out her phone, snapped a photo, and then showed me the screen. "Here."

"God, you know me so well." Sure as hell, Mikki wasn't lying. Something about those words reached into my chest and squeezed. But I didn't have time to ponder those thoughts.

"Here you go." The server reappeared with our drinks and hotdogs. "Also brought you some pretzels, nachos, and popcorn. All of the stadium favorites." She handed food trays to each of us.

"I'm in love with you," Stella proclaimed as she dipped her pretzel into the nacho cheese. "Thank you."

"No problem." She held out one last container and opened it to us. It was a small divided bowl filled with condiments, relish, onions, and shredded cheese. We each helped ourselves, loading our hotdogs full. "If you need anything else, just wave to me, my name is Andi, I'll be right over there." She pointed to an offset area that was out of the way, but close enough that she could still easily watch the area.

We turned and got comfy in our seats as the crowd started to get restless. "They're getting ready to come out." Mikki stomped her feet.

"How do you know?" I asked between bites.

"The auxiliary staff is coming out. See." She pointed to a few men and women meandering on to the court and making their way over to folding chairs that were behind another row of chairs and off to the side of the players' bench.

A bead of sweat rolled down my back, and my heart felt as if I had a murmur with erratic rhythms. I sat forward, my knees bobbing. "You nervous?" Stella whispered.

"No. I don't know. What if I'm handling this all wrong?"

"You aren't. Calm down and enjoy the ride wherever it takes you."

My knees were well into a cantor as the sports announcer called out the Celtics eight bench warmers followed by their starting lineup.

Then it came to the Lightning. Mikki grabbed my arm and pulled me up. I counted player after player as they ran to the center and shook hands with each of the Celtic players.

"And tonight's starting lineup, let's hear it for your home team, Lightning." The announcer called out a name, then another, and another. I was holding my breath when he finally called, "Shooting guard number thirty-three Aaron Skkye." The announcer began another name, but I didn't listen, I only had eyes for one person.

He ran forward, but his eyes were locked on me. Suddenly, I felt shy. I waved, and a wide smile spread across his lips. A scuffle in the audience threatened to steal my attention, but I didn't want to turn my head and risk breaking our eye contact.

"Jesus Christ, Vivian, the crowd is going crazy trying to figure out who he is looking at, who is making him smile so brightly." Mikki shoved my shoulder with hers.

My attention snapped to her. "What?" Then I glanced around to find several people were staring at me, others staring in our direction but not sure exactly where.

I faced forward and leaned back, contemplating what I was going to do.

"Right there, what I saw proves it all, you're crazy about him, and the feeling is clearly mutual." Stella grabbed my hand. "Enjoy it, hell, enjoy him."

Andi appeared with three takeout-style boxes. "I thought you might like these." She handed one to each of us with a spoon.

We opened them while she collected our garbage.

"Red velvet cake? I'm in heaven."

"Have I told you I love you?" Stella asked before she shoved a large bite into her mouth.

"Thank you. Let me know when you're ready for refills."

"Will do, thank you." I smiled at her as she slid back into her small space.

With cake in hand, the three of us sat at the edge of our seats and watched tip-off, where the ball was tossed into the air and the tallest players jumped to hit and others were ready to grab it if it was headed their way.

The men were off, dribbling and passing the ball from person to person, moving closer to the basket until Aaron took control of it.

"Yes," I shouted when Aaron shot the ball and it landed in the basket. When it came down, a Celtics player snagged the ball and they bounced it, passed, and slowly worked it toward the opposite side of the court.

"Way to go Gage," Mikki shouted.

"What did I miss?"

"That's Gage Armentrout, number nineteen, he recouped the ball for us, see?" Mikki pointed to the court, and I finally realized that the Lightning did indeed have the ball again.

The buzzer rang and Aaron ran and joined his team huddled together, but not before he looked over at me and smiled.

I nodded back, letting him know he absolutely had my full attention, and then I glanced around as more people were staring at me, sure that I was the one making Aaron Skkye smile.

The buzzer sounded again and the players moved down the court.

"I wonder what's going on?" Mikki pointed toward a woman who was running out of the tunnel and toward the Lightning team side. "That's Carmen Romero."

"The owner?" I asked, studying the woman who owned an entire friggin' basketball team.

"Yep."

She whispered into the head coach's ear. He stepped forward, blew his whistle, and called a time-out. "Skkye, over here."

It was as if the entire stadium leaned forward to try to hear, as if that were even possible.

I leaned forward too, hoping to hear something, but it was futile. So, I watched his face, and what I saw there had my stomach twisting in worry. Aaron said something to the two people in front of him, they both nodded, and he ran off the court, not looking back, not acknowledging me.

"What just happened?" Stella asked.

"I have no clue." Whatever it was couldn't have been good, not with the way he'd taken off.

"You want to go?" she asked.

"Let's wait a few." I reached for my phone to see if there was a text, but there weren't any. So, I texted him.

ME: Are you okay? Can I help?

I WAITED for bubbles to appear, but by the time the second quarter finished and halftime began, he hadn't responded.

"Can we go now?" I asked softly.

"Sure, come on." Stella stood, and to my great relief, Mikki did too without any push back.

None of us said a word as we walked up the stairs and passed Andi. I paused to reach into my purse and grab a twenty for a tip.

She placed her hand on mine. "No need, Mr. Skkye took care of it. I hope that everything is okay."

"Thank you, me too."

It was weird. I saw him leave, I knew that he was okay, but still there was something so ominous about tonight.

"Are you the woman who has captured Aaron Skkye's attention?" A microphone was thrust toward me, hitting Stella in the process.

"Excuse me? You just hit me."

"Sorry," the woman said without an ounce of apology.

"Please leave," Mikki snapped.

"I just want an answer," Haley Loles demanded, as if I would give the reporter I had to deal with during Eric's case and despised with a passion, an answer.

The vapid bitch probably didn't even remember who I was or how much pain she'd caused me a few years ago.

Stella leaned into Hayley's face. "Well you aren't getting one. Let's get an officer over here so he can assist us out of here and maybe take out the trash along the way. Maybe we can even talk about pressing charges for assault since you hit me with your fucking mic."

"I seriously doubt an officer will care about something so petty." She smirked. "Plus, I'm just doing my job."

"Being a bitch? You excel at it. But I think they will care about harassing us." Stella glanced around. "Hey, Max, can you come over here?" Stella hollered to Max Longoria, an off-duty deputy who was picking up some overtime working at the stadium. "This reporter blocked Vivian from leaving, thrust her microphone in her face, hit me with it, and now is saying no one will care what she does. We want to leave."

"I'll take care of it. Why, Haley Loles, we meet again. You have a special fondness for cops, don't you?" Max chuckled. We all knew how much she hated law enforcement, but it was okay because the feeling was mutual.

I didn't talk, not on the ride to Sixes, not when Stella or

Mikki asked questions. When we got back to the bar, I headed to my car and drove home.

Media, fucking media. I hated them. I had to deal with them after Eric died. They constantly followed me, refusing to let me grieve in my own way. They called me Orlando's sweetheart. They constantly questioned me about my feelings, how I was doing, and then checked in for weeks afterward to catch everyone up on Orlando's sweetheart, widow of slain officer, Sergeant Eric Haines. When I wouldn't talk to them because I just wanted to be left alone in my own pity party, they started using threats. I could hear them all over again, it would be all too easy to ruin Eric's name, everyone thinks so highly of him, I would hate to see that change. Every morning I would open the paper and scour the headlines to see if there was any vile word.

I checked my phone for what had to be the fiftieth time but still nothing.

AARON

I was home only long enough to change and pack a bag. I had called my assistant for help finding me a flight, but the next one wasn't until tomorrow midmorning, which was too late. I needed to get there faster. I pulled my Cayenne out of the garage and headed north, back to Evansville, Indiana, a place I hadn't been since graduating early at seventeen, and leaving seven years ago when I got a full ride to the University of Kentucky.

"Ireland has been in an accident," Carmen had whispered.

I'd thought about Ireland almost every day for the last seven years, wondering if she was doing well, but it wasn't my place, not anymore, hadn't been since the second I signed those adoption papers.

How I wished I could do something more than anonymously sending her gifts she would never know were from me.

"Aaron, you need to go, head to Evansville, Indiana." Carmen had never sounded so serious. "The three of them were in a car accident, only Ireland survived. They are contacting you as the biological father." Carmen rubbed my back. "Are you okay?"

I kept driving up I-75 until I finally hit Chattanooga, Tennessee, and then I merged on to I-24, only when I had to.

I was a hundred and twenty miles outside of Evansville when Heidi called. "Good morning, Heidi."

"Good morning, Aaron. I've made a reservation for you at the Double Tree; it appears to be the nicest hotel in the area."

"Fine, anything is fine."

"The reservation is open ended, so there's no rush. I spoke with Miss Romero, and she said to take your time. Is there anything else you need from me?"

My skin slowly changed to white as I squeezed my knuckles around the steering wheel. Did I have Heidi do it or not? "Can you do me a favor?"

"Of course."

"I'd normally never ask for something like this, send some gorgeous flowers to Vivian, she owns Sixes Bar & Grille. Just write, I'm sorry, an emergency arose. Love, Aaron."

"Love? Wow, that's something I've never written for you before."

"Goodbye, Heidi, I'll call if I need anything else."

"Goodbye, sir."

Two hours later, I crossed the bridge into Evansville, hit the map link Heidi had sent, and followed the directions to my hotel.

I pulled up to valet; it was always easier to have my car waiting as soon as I hurried out of a hotel than to have to walk to it with people following me and taking pictures or asking for photographs.

The valet wasn't much over eighteen. He opened my door and froze staring at me. "Umm, hello Mr. Skkye."

"Shhh, let's not make a big deal of this, okay?"

He nodded, and I reached into my backseat and grabbed

my hanger-bag with all of my clothes and my toiletry bag. He handed me my ticket, I handed him a twenty, and then I headed for the front desk.

Before I made it there, a woman in a polyester business suit that had to be itchy as fuck intercepted me.

"Welcome, Mr. Skkye, I'm Jenny Winternheimer, the general manager. We already have your room ready. Your assistant has given a card to be put on file. You are on the top floor, corner suite, here is your key. May we help you with your luggage?"

"No thanks, I've got it."

"Would you like some breakfast sent up?"

"That would be awesome. Whatever they can do fast is great, I'm not picky."

"We're on it."

"Thank you so much, Ms. Win . . . Jenny."

She laughed. "Winternheimer, but don't worry, hardly anyone gets it right the first time. Here's my card, let me know if you need anything while you are with us."

I took her card and headed for the elevators, Winternheimer . . . hmmm. Now that she mentioned it, I remember going to school with a lot of unique names, just never thought about them being German: Niemeier, Wimpleberg, Winzapfel, Snodgrass. That last one still caught me off guard, that name was a hard no for me.

There was a large basket of fresh fruit waiting for me inside my suite. I hung up my garment bag then grabbed a banana before moving the lock on my door and setting it so it wouldn't latch and the room service waiter could come on in. Then I started making phone calls.

"Thank you for calling the Vanderburgh county department of Children and Family Services, we open at nine a.m., please call back during our normal time, or in the case of an emergency, please call eight-one-two . . ." I wrote down the number and then hung up.

Dialing the next number, I waited.

"Hello?"

"Hi, this is Aaron Skkye, some—"

"Oh, Aaron, I'm so glad you called. It's me, Karen Koehler —well, you would remember me as Karen Kingsland. We went to high school together. I'm the one who called you. I know it isn't proper protocol, but I saw the file when we were alerted about the girl and knew instantly who she was. Evansville still isn't that big; we know everyone's business. I remembered you and Maisy having that baby." Good god, when would this woman shut up? I didn't need to be reminded about things I already knew.

"What about seeing—"

"Anyway, she's alone and there were no other next of kin, so I contacted you. When can you get to Evansville?"

"I'm here already."

"Oh. Well then. She just had surgery—"

"Why? On what?"

"On her wrist, she needed it set."

"Can I see her?"

"Well . . . ummm . . . we're not sure she even knows that she was adopted. We need to go very carefully here. Since I'm the one handling Ireland's case, I need to ask if you have heard from Maisy or know of her whereabouts?"

"No. Not once since she snuck out of the hospital. I have no clue where she is or even if she is still alive."

"That's too bad."

"Tell me about it. I never understood her leaving." I glanced up as my door opened, and waved for the waiter to carry in my tray. Like the valet, he paused and stared for a second.

I reached for the black cheque folder to sign the bill.

"It's taken care of," Troy, according to his name tag, said.

After I handed him a ten, he closed the door behind himself as he left, and I made a mental note to get cash.

"Let's meet at Deaconess hospital at two o'clock, is that okay with you?"

"Sure, why not before?"

"I'm meeting the doctor at three, I'd like to talk with you, and then if we come to a consensus, you can listen as well. I'll meet you at the main entrance."

I hung up, set my alarm for twelve thirty and then turned to eat before taking a much-needed nap.

AARON

Sorry, John Mellencamp, but your idea of living in a small town and mine are two totally different things.

I thumped my steering wheel as I drove down Mary Street on the way to the hospital.

My mind was whirling, could I do this? Of course I could, there was no other choice. The times I spent in foster care, when my mom was picked up and someone thought to look to see if she had any kids at home, were nightmarish. It wasn't just that I was young and scared, either. There was always something cold about those places, no matter how hard they tried to make them feel otherwise.

There was no way I would allow my daughter to even spend a minute in foster care.

Turning down the radio when the large building came into sight, my knuckles popped as I flexed them to turn into the parking lot. Getting out of my Porsche Cayenne, the first thing I spied was a woman who had to be in her early forties bundled up in one of those huge parachute material puffy monstrosities. There was no way I went to high school with her. Maybe Karen had something come up.

"Aaron, it's been a long time." The woman stepped in to give me a big hug. "It's me, Karen." She pulled back. "You haven't changed one bit."

"Thanks. How have you been?"

"Oh, you know, I've been good. I'm a mom—oh, and I married Buck Koehler, you two played basketball together. Remember him?"

Holy shit, where were the batteries to turn this thing off?

"I do." Buck had been the biggest asshole on Earth. Every time he thought I showed him up, he'd pull some stupid prank and think it was funny as hell.

"Come on, it is way too cold to be standing outside. We have a small conference room waiting for us." Karen began walking and I was left to follow as she continued chattering. "Well, you are just famous here. Have you been over to Reitz High School yet? Oh, of course not, you just got in. But you should, they have your jersey up in a case along with some of your photos and the team's photos the years you all won State Championship. Mater Dei is still our biggest rival around here, nothing like good ole westside rivalry, huh?"

"Yeah." I kept my head down as we maneuvered through the hospital to a small room. My mind was on Ireland and trying not to vomit as the overpowering smells hit me: it was a mixture of disinfectants, cleaners, and just that nondescript smell of sick people.

"Here we go." Karen set her bag on a table and then began removing the overstuffed parachute burrito. "All right, let's get to business."

Her manner changed, and she turned into a caseworker. I was pleasantly surprised to see that I wasn't going to have to put up with the insane garble any longer. "First, as I'm sure you know, Ireland Kelly Lacy is seven years old as of—"

"September nineteenth, yeah, I know."

"Both her parents were only children, and according to

information relayed by Judge Lacy's assistant, there were no other family members. She did inform us that there is a directive filed so she is trying to get that for us."

"Judge?"

"Yes, Ryan Lacy was a circuit court judge, he handled traffic court, and his wife, Shannon, was a stay-at-home mom who homeschooled Ireland. I contacted you because Ireland has very few options unfortunately, but ultimately my goal is to make foster care the last option. I'll try every possible alternative, and you are it. What I need to know is whether you are in a position to assume custody of your biological daughter."

"I am." It was weird because there was no stutter or no second to hesitate. The answer just flew out. "She's mine. I have the means to take care of her."

"Very well then. There will be forms to fill out, and we'll need to meet with a judge who handles these cases. Because I'm assuming you are going to want to take her back to where you live?" Karen pulled out a huge folder and handled it over to me.

"Of course, my job is there. I'd like to get an attorney to help go through the paperwork with me."

"I can—"

Karen was cut off by a knock at the door and in walked a doctor. He had that white circle of hair that looked like a snow crown, while the top of his head was bald. Why not just shave it at this point, has anyone told him how stupid that looked?

"Mrs. Koehler, may we speak?" the doctor asked.

"Doctor Lewis, this is Aaron Skkye." I stood to shake the man's hand. "He will be Ireland's temporary guardian until the courts make a ruling," Karen explained.

"Very well. Ireland is doing remarkable considering what she's been through. She broke her radius and fractured her ulna, so we set the bones. The radius required a pin to move it up to the scaphoid. Surgery went well, but she did sustain a concussion, so we would like to keep an eye on her a little longer. Do you all have any questions for me?"

"Nope, I think we've got it," Karen answered.

"I do. How is she emotionally right now, has anyone told her?"

"Yes, she knows they are deceased, she was locked in the car with them until rescue could cut her out. She is how you would expect after learning of such stuff," The doctor answered.

I turned to Karen and whispered, "She is how is expected... How can anyone expect this? She's a kid. I can't imagine being locked in a car after both of my parents had just been killed."

"Neither can I, which is why we need to be very delicate with how we proceed. She's seen more than someone her age ever should, and the ramifications of that could manifest in a number of different ways."

The doctor looked thoughtful for a second before adding, "Before we discharge her, I will make sure to pass along some referrals for child psychologists who specialize in these kinds of situations."

"Thanks."

The doctor left, and after a moment, Karen offered me a soft smile. "Do you want to go see her?"

"I would love that."

"Then let's go, but please remember that we aren't sure if she knows that she was adopted so we need to move gingerly on this, okay?"

Karen handed me a visitor's badge and then led me through the hospital. On our way, I shot off a handful of texts to Heidi, asking her to find me a family law attorney, and she assured me she would get right on it.

After what felt like a three-mile-long walk, Karen came to a stop in front of a room. The wall was glass, and the curtains were pulled for privacy, but I knew that Ireland was inside. Karen was the first to enter, and I lagged behind taking a few deep breaths before following.

"Hello, Ireland, I brought someone here to meet you. This is—"

Ireland's eyes widened for a second with happiness and then with hurt. "I know who you are. You're Aaron Skkye, my dad and I used to watch basketball together all the time. He used to tell me about you."

I thought that drills made my heart race, a game in overtime weighed on me, but nothing compared to this . . . she was beautiful. Her dark brown hair was wavy just like mine, but her bright blue eyes were all Maisy.

"Hi, Ireland." Moving nearer, I pulled a chair up next to her and took a seat. "What else do you know about me?"

"I know that you're my birth father, but you gave me up for adoption. My parents wanted me. I want my parents." Ireland started crying.

"Can you leave us for a few minutes?" I asked Karen, and she patted my shoulder like some older mother figure.

"I've got calls to make. I'll be back in that conference room if you need me, okay?" I nodded and she left.

"I know you do, I'm so sorry this has happened to you."

"Really? Then why wasn't it you? You didn't want me in the first place, they did. You gave me up. Now you're here, and they're gone, and I have no one. It isn't fair." Ireland wailed. She wasn't wanting for me to say anything, so I stayed silent. "What's going to happen to me? My mom and dad were all I had." Her tears were falling hard as she tried with a valiant effort to pull herself together, but she just couldn't. "I want my parents!" Ireland shouted.

"That's why I'm here."

81

Ireland shook her head, "No, that's my problem; I want my mom, not you. Please, get my mom for me, she's at home, she's waiting for me, I know she is. My dad is just at work, that's all, he's at work, he'll be home soon. Tell me this was all a nightmare, please, please."

I fought my own urge to cry as I listened to her go through every possibility until she finally accepted the truth about what had happened. It didn't matter, I was going to be here for her, never again would she be alone.

"I'm going home." Ireland moved the covers back but winced at the pain.

"Stop Ireland, you have to stay here a little longer."

"But I'm alone here."

"I'll stay with you as long as you want."

"I don't want you. You don't want me," Ireland lashed out.

"Yes, I do, I want you with all of my soul." It was true, I really did want her, she had always held a special place in my heart.

"Why? You didn't want me when I was born. It was why you gave me away."

I trailed one hand down my sleep-deprived face. "That isn't true. I've always wanted you, but sometimes, it is more important to think of others than it is to think of yourself."

"I don't even know what to call you, what are you to me besides my biological father? I'm not going to call you that."

"How about Aaron, you call me Aaron, and I'll call you Ireland."

Ireland stared at me. "Are you being forced to take me now, you know, because I'm all alone?"

I grabbed a chair and pulled it up so I could sit next to her bed. I held her uninjured hand in mine, and it was tiny compared to my giant one. "I've always wanted you. I've thought about you every day. On September nineteenth—"

"Hey, that's my birthday."

"I know, and every year on that date, all I can think about is you and what type of person you're growing up to be. I wonder if you're happy and if you love your life as much as I hoped you would. Every day, I regret that I wasn't able to be the parent you needed me to be back then, but I also know that your parents loved you and were able to give you the life I couldn't have."

"Really?"

"Really. It was what was best for you, and you were the only thing that mattered to me. I was just a kid, I hadn't graduated high school, and I didn't have a good home to go to."

"Why?"

"I will tell you about that another time, okay?"

Ireland nodded.

"What about my biological mom?"

"Her name was Maisy, you have the same exact eyes as her, they're beautiful. Maisy wasn't happy giving up her teenage years."

"In this same hospital, right?" Ireland asked.

"Yep, you were born in this very hospital." I took a deep breath and recomposed myself. "I followed the nurses. I thought you were the most beautiful thing ever in the world. You were amazing, you had ten fingers and ten toes. I couldn't believe that you were just perfect." Ireland smiled brightly at my words. "By the time I made my way back down to Maisy's room, she was gone."

"What do you mean gone? Where did she go?"

I shrugged my shoulders. "Don't know. The security guards pulled up the video from the cameras that showed her leaving, but no one has seen or heard from her again. She just disappeared." Ireland sat quietly, absorbing everything I had just told her. "That's why I decided it was best to give you to the Lacys; they wanted a baby so bad and would be so good to you. It was just me, and I had no way to take care of you. As much as it broke my heart—and I mean broke, smashed it to pieces—I signed the papers because it was best for you. And you were the only one who mattered to me.

Ireland closed her eyes. I waited and waited. When she didn't reopen them, I found it a great time to go find Karen.

I walked out to the nurses' station and waited for the woman behind the desk to glance up at me. "If Ireland wakes up and wants to know where I am, just tell her that I went to talk with Karen. I'll be back."

"No problem, Mr. Skkye."

AARON

"What's up, boss?" Heidi asked.

"Tell me you have something, anything, I just need direction."

"I do. You are meeting with an attorney named Jameson Lane at the offices of Tuttle and Lane at six o'clock, and you are paying double the normal hourly rate for the late time."

"Of course I am."

"I'll text you directions," Heidi stated.

I took a long, slow breath, trying to assure myself that this would all work out. "Thanks, Heidi, remind me to give you a bonus."

"Oh, I will, don't worry." She disconnected, and I continued on my way to find Karen.

Opening the door to the conference room, I found her bent over stacks of papers and a file folder opened with Ireland's name written along the top.

"So, how did everything go with Ireland?" Karen asked as she shuffled papers together.

"Great, we had a little heart-to-heart; she's really worried about what is going to happen to her."

Karen reached forward and patted my hand. "Don't take it as her being self-centered, this is normal. Children need boundaries, and they need to know that they belong. All of that has just been ripped from her and she doesn't know what is going to happen. She's establishing where she belongs."

"Oh, I could never think that beautiful girl was self-centered. She is curious and worried, that's all."

"Anything else?"

"My assistant set up a meeting for me with an attorney for this evening at six. I'm going to leave since it's already after five and then go back to my hotel. What time do visiting hours begin tomorrow?"

"Nine. I'll be here. I've sent papers to the judge who has been assigned to this case. I'm hoping that he will look at it even though it's the weekend and not wait until Monday. I hate the thought of Ireland going into foster care when you're here."

"No, let me watch her," I demanded.

"It doesn't work like that, just know I'm trying, okay?"

I nodded, but I wasn't happy about it.

As I made my way back out to the parking lot, I contemplated going to find the judge myself since he was probably just on some golf course. After a second, I dismissed it. Pissing off the person who had total control over where my daughter went was a terrible idea.

I'd let my attorney do it.

I got into my car and followed the GPS directions to the attorney's office.

It was a brick building that looked just like the buildings to its left and right. It had a dark brown roof and dark wood fascia. The whole thing looked like something from *That 70s Show*. I parked along the curb.

Getting out of my car, I heard a gasp from a guy walking

to his car but ignored him as I walked up the small flight of steps and opened the door, which was also dark brown —shocking.

A brunette, a man-eating brunette in a dress that was almost too sexy for work, waved for me to join her as she stood from a table in a glass-walled conference room. As I neared, she immediately began speaking. "Mr. Skkye, I'm Jameson Lane. Have a seat."

She pointed to a chair opposite her. "I'm so glad you could make it; this will give me the weekend to do some research and get my ducks in a row. I hope it wasn't too much trouble."

"None at all. Let's get started, we have a lot to go over."

"First, I need you to sign these." She slid a attorney-client privilege information act form in front of me along with a contract. "Your assistant has already received a copy of both as well."

I snagged my phone and sent a text to Heidi. I trusted no one when it came to contracts.

ME: The legal contract for this attorney?

Heidi: Dan read over it, standard protocol nothing hidden. Sign.

I PUT my phone away relieved that Heidi had gotten Dan, the team's contract attorney, to review it for me on such short notice. I signed both and then handed them back over, waiting for what was next.

"First thing I'm going to do is contact Judge Lacy's chambers and see what paperwork he may have had on file. Being who he was, I'm sure he had a final will and testament, and his assistant probably knows where that is. I'll also get in contact with Judge Martin Cree, he'll be the one to oversee this case; we need to get an immediate ruling for temporary guardianship under extenuating circumstances."

"What do I need to do?" I asked, totally blown away by this woman's plan of action.

"Right now, nothing."

"How long do you think it will take for the judge to rule on temporary guardianship?"

"It's Friday so he'll be going to Petroleum Club with his wife." Petroleum Club was a members only restaurant, and you could only get a membership if you were willing to pay thousands of dollars for it. When I was a teenager, the assholes in school would talk about eating there, as if they had dined in New York. "But tomorrow, he will be on the green, so I'll catch him around the eighteenth hole."

"That's it?" I asked.

"That's it. Just wait for my call, telling you that you can take the child—"

"Ireland."

"I'm sorry, what?" Jameson was perplexed.

"You said child; her name is Ireland."

"Oh, yes. I'll let you know when you can take custodial guardianship of Ireland. But be ready, I'm sure we will have to meet the judge on Monday or Tuesday."

"No problem." I rose and extended a hand. We shook, and I let out a sigh of relief. This was all going to be okay. I had just gotten into my car when my phone rang.

Assuming it was Heidi, I answered. "Yes?"

"What the fuck happened? Where are you? I went by your house and your Aston was in the garage, but the Porsche was gone."

"Whoa, Gage. First, glad to know that key I gave you in case of emergencies is useful."

"Yeah, well, if you had thought to send your best friend a

text, I wouldn't have had to try to hunt you down to try to get my wife off my case. She's been freaking the fuck out ever since you ran out at the timeout, because she didn't know what the hell happened."

"Remember when I told you about me being a teenage father?"

"Yeah, and you gave her up for adoption. What about her?"

"Her adoptive parents were killed in a car crash."

"And your daughter?"

"She has a broken wrist, but other than that, she's good."

"Wow, so why were you contacted?"

"She has no other family at all, so I'm going to get her back."

"You mean—"

"I mean, I have a daughter, and she is coming home with me to live, permanently."

"Whoa." Gage let out a deep breath. "Whoa."

"Anything else you have to say besides whoa?"

"Not sure there is anything else except congratulations."

"Thanks."

"Just wait until LeeAnn finds out."

"Gage, tell her not to tell anyone else just yet. I trust you two and would never ask you to keep something from your wife, but no one else, okay?"

"You got it. We're here if you need us."

I disconnected just as I was pulling up to the valet. He took my keys, and I pocketed the ticket as I made my way up to my room.

Only, once I got there, I was too restless to relax. I paced the room, sat, watched some television, and sat again. Finally glancing at the nightstand clock, I saw it was just after twelve, it was the time when Vivian and I normally spoke. I couldn't believe it had only been a day, one single fucking day. Biting the bullet, I snagged my phone and dialed.

"Oh my god, Aaron, are you okay?"

"Hi, Little One, yes, I'm fine."

"What happened?" The sound of Vivian's voice was so soothing to my tangled up brain.

"There was an emergency, and I had to come up to Indiana. I'm sorry for abandoning you after I asked to take you home."

"Oh stop, that's no biggie, it's you I'm worried about. Is everything okay?"

"It will be now that I have it under control."

"Do you want to talk about it? I'm a great listener."

"When I get back home, I'll tell you all about it; it's too big to talk about over the phone."

"Okay. When do you think you'll be back?"

"Tuesday or Wednesday."

"Just call me if you need anything." Vivian was always so kind. I had no clue what to do. Ireland needed me and was probably going to need my full attention for some time while she acclimated. Would a woman fit into the mix, especially a skittish one who already had her own baggage? I hadn't realized it until a sharp pain penetrated my scalp and then pulling my fingers from my head, I saw a clump of hair. Great, I was pulling at my hair. I was sure Sigmund Freud had some psychological diagnosis for this—something like, pulling hair is the stage right before patient enters catatonia.

SATURDAY MORNING I WOKE, somewhat refreshed, and was headed up to the hospital. I swung through the Donut Bank, got some things I thought Ireland might like, and grabbed a few crullers for me. I was standing at the nurses' station, trying to ignore the women at eight fifty-five—five minutes before official start of visitation time—and they weren't letting me go a second earlier. When the recorded voice came across the overhead intercom, welcoming people to Deaconess hospital, I marched forward and into Ireland's room.

"You're back." Ireland appeared more relieved than shocked.

"Yep, I'm back. I'm not going anywhere. You're stuck with me." I glanced over at her breakfast tray. "Not hungry?"

"That's crap."

"Crap? Are you allowed to say crap?" I asked and instantly realized my mistake as Ireland's face changed. "Hey, I brought donuts." I held up the bag.

"What kind? Did you get any Tiger Tails?"

I handed her the bag, knowing full well there were two in there, thank god, and waited for the bag to come back so I could grab my donuts.

"So, you might get out of here today?"

She nodded, as if she had already known that. "Where will I go?"

"I'm not sure yet, but I'm hoping it's with me. I hired an attorney who is trying to get a judge to sign papers that will let me take you out of the hospital."

"What if he won't let you? Where will I go?"

"To some friends of Miss Karen's but just for a night or two."

Tears welled in Ireland's eyes. "But I don't want to go to their house, I don't know them."

"It will only be for a day or two." I wanted to promise her it would only be for that long, but fear stopped me. No matter how much I wanted to, I knew better than to make a promise I wasn't sure I would be able to keep.

"Would I have my own bedroom?"

"Probably not, but it will be safe."

"I'm not going. I want to go home to my house on Koring Road."

"I'm trying, Ireland, I can't promise."

"Then get out. Get out. I don't want to see you. Out. Out." A nurse came running in to see what all the shouting was about.

"Ireland, what's wrong, sweetheart?" She moved me out of the way.

"I want to be left alone." She folded her arms across her chest and let out a long huff.

"Maybe it would be best if you came back later," the nurse whispered to me.

I conceded, but not before locking eyes with my daughter. I wanted her to feel the love I had for her, had always had for her.

Leaving the room, I ran smack dab into Karen.

"Hey, got a second?" Karen asked.

"Yeah, but we should probably go to the conference room."

"Is Ireland all right?"

"I don't know. She told me to leave."

"She doesn't mean it; she's going through a myriad of emotions right now. It's important that, whatever you do, you don't leave her alone too much. She needs to know she isn't alone, even if she just hears you moving close to her." Karen paused and looked around for a second. "Here, follow me." She led me down the hall to a small room and knocked on the door. When no one answered, she opened it and took a seat. I did the same. "How are you doing? Are you positive about this?"

"Absolutely. When I gave up my rights, I wasn't in a good place, and it was probably the best thing I could have done for her. But I'm not a scared, broke kid anymore."

She smiled warmly. "No, you aren't, and I'm proud of you for showing up like you did."

"Did you think I wouldn't come?"

"I hoped you would, but when you do what I do for a living and see what I see, sometimes you never know."

I lived through some of the nightmares Karen had probably seen, and while she might remember enough of the gossip to think to call me when Ireland's name landed on her desk, there was no way she could fathom the extent of the neglect I had suffered as a kid. It wasn't something I liked to talk about.

"Did you know her adoptive parents?" I asked, hoping that she had.

"I didn't. Why?"

"I need to find out about her parents' final wishes. I was online yesterday Googling about what children go through and one page talked all about regrets, the regrets people had about not getting to say goodbye to their parent because someone kept them away from the funeral when they were a kid. I don't want Ireland to feel that way."

"I'm really happy to see you taking that initiative. Your attorney will be able to find that out. I brought you a list of names just in case the one yesterday didn't work out." Karen reached for her bag.

"No, the attorney was great, I hired her. She is trying to get a copy of the Lacys' will and contact Judge Cree."

"Who did you hire?"

"Jameson Lane."

Karen's eyes widened. "You got the best; she is a shark."

"What's next?" I folded my hands and rested them on the table as if praying.

"I'll file papers with the state on Monday. The first part of this is very quick, it is where they declare you her temporary guardian and a thirty-day wait period begins. During that time, if anyone has proof of why they should be the legal guardian of Ireland and comes forward then there will be a hearing. The rest is drawn out and may require you to come back for a meeting or two with the judge, but let's get through this first step before we worry about that, okay?"

"I'm okay with that, whatever I need to do."

"Aaron, I know that you want this, and I believe that you are what's right for Ireland, now we just need to convince the judge of that. I need to go chat with Ireland and try to find out if they are releasing her today." Karen got up and left the small room.

AARON

$\mathcal{I}$ nearly dropped my phone on the hard terrazzo floor when it rang while I was staring at Vivian's texts and having a pity party. Not recognizing the number but knowing that it was from this area, I answered anyway.

"Hello?"

"Where are you?" a woman asked, I didn't recognize the voice.

I answered somewhat reluctantly. "At Deaconess hospital."

"Okay, but where, that's sort of a big building."

"Pediatric unit."

"I have no ever-loving clue where that is."

"Who is this?" I finally asked.

"Oh, sorry. This is Jameson, your attorney."

"I'm on the fourth floor in a private conference room."

"Hold that room, I'll be there shortly.

"Okay . . ."

She disconnected, and I was left staring at a black screen, no explanation, no anything. It wasn't even five minutes later that she walked in wearing a bright red golf skirt and a low-cut, white golf shirt.

"You aren't going to believe what I got." She shook her large bag at me.

"Obviously, you met the judge at the eighteenth hole."

"Yes, and he was shocked to find out Ryan had been killed. The names haven't been released yet, because they weren't sure who the next of kin was and were waiting to notify them." Jameson took a seat at the small table and began spreading out her papers. "After I told him, he informed me that Judge Lacy had all of his affairs in order as well as an entire estate plan, including guardianship of Ireland according to Judge Cree. He said that he was the one to personally notarize it for Ryan Lacy."

"Okay, who is the guardian?"

"You are." Jameson pulled a reddish-brown legal file in front of her, opened it, and then unclipped a letter that was fastened to the front before handing it to me.

I took the envelope with the judge's seal up in one corner and opened it, not sure why he would leave me a letter.

Unfolding the letter, I read:

AARON,

If you're reading this, obviously, something has happened to my wife and me. When we first met you, I saw in you something that I admired; I could tell that you were torn over what was right for Ireland. In the end, I believe you did what was best, and we are thankful for the years we've had with her.

You were just a child yourself, you never had what you wanted Ireland to have. So many times, my wife and I wanted to invite you to come live with us, but I was afraid, not that you would take Ireland or anything, but that you wouldn't leave. You would cherish having the family you never had and pass up the opportunity of a lifetime, your scholarship and chance to play in the NBA.

I went to some of your University of Kentucky games, and I tried to make it whenever you played the Pacers. Each time I saw you on the court, I knew I had made the right choice. I'm proud of you and proud of the man you've become despite how you grew up. Which leads me to the big request, please take Ireland. We have no one else, and I know that you love her and never forgot about her.

The mystery gifts that arrived every September nineteenth weren't such a mystery. It wasn't hard to guess you'd sent them. She knows all about you, we've always been open with her, and I know that with time, she will understand why you did what you did and find appreciation for it.

I know that you can provide for her and love her. Please think hard on this for us, for Ireland.

Ryan and Shannon Lacy

I REFOLDED the letter and slid it back into the envelope. My mind was whirling as I tried to process so much information. I glanced up at Jameson, who was reading a document as well. When she finished, she had a wide smile spread across her face.

"What did the letter say?" Jameson asked.

"He asked if I'd take Ireland."

"And . . ."

"Of course I will; it's what I want."

"Then you just need to sign here." She slid the document she had just been reading over to me. "He already had filled out everything. You are now the temporary legal guardian for Ireland Lacy."

"Why not permanent?"

"You'll still have to make an appearance in Juvenile Probate so Judge McCree can make it legally binding and have it entered into the records."

She pulled a sealed nine-by-twelve envelope out of her file folder and opened it. "This is Mr. and Mrs. Lacy's will." Jameson flipped through the pages and quickly scanned everything, before turning her eyes back to me.

"Basically, everything is left to you if you take Ireland. If you decide not to take Ireland, they ask that you be the trustee and portion out funds to whoever takes care of her when she's eighteen, twenty-one, and the remaining amount at twenty-five."

"I'm taking her, but I don't want anything, it's hers, all hers. I have my own money." I was more than financially stable enough to take care of my daughter.

"Then do what they asked you to do for anyone else and put it in a trust for her." Jameson's phone dinged and she looked at it, scrolling through the text. "That was Judge Cree's assistant; we are meeting him Monday at ten fifteen in his chambers. Karen Koehler will speak with the judge first and then we will. Ireland must attend." Jameson leaned forward and placed one hand on top of mine. "Don't look so worried, if you are positive that you're ready for this then it is a done deal. We should have this wrapped up in a few days." She pulled her hand back.

"Was there anything in there that stipulated their final wishes, like funeral or cremation?" I asked, hoping that if the Lacys had enough forethought to set this up, then they had taken care of final wishes as well.

"There is." Jameson handed me a thick legal envelope marked Oak Lawn Cemetery, which I tucked into my inside front breast pocket to read later.

"We will meet at a quarter to ten Monday morning in the front of the courthouse." Jameson began sliding everything back into her satchel. "Here's my card, call if you need anything. This is pretty much a closed case, since they appointed you as her guardian and you are her birth father, so it is very unlikely the judge will contradict their wishes. Oh, I forgot to give you this." Jameson pulled out another envelope that was bulging with something inside.

I opened it and found several keys. "What are these for?"

"His assistant told me they are copies to everything the Lacys owned. Bank deposit, safe, house, cars, everything. All of the other important information is inside."

"Do you come across many people this organized?"

"No, why do you ask?" Jameson raised a brow, studying me.

"I don't know . . . it's almost like he knew something was going to happen to them or something."

"Maybe he just saw the nightmare some people go through when a loved one passes away without leaving their affairs in order. The man was also anal retentive. He left his office every day at exactly five after five. He started his sessions on the hour and not a minute late. I think it was just him."

"Okay." I let it go. "Thank you so much for rushing up here with all of this."

"No problem, I have to get copies over to the DCF so they know you have legal temporary guardianship."

"Karen's here. She's with Ireland."

"Great, let's go see if we can find her."

I held open the door for her and then pointed to the right. "That way," I said, knowing she had no clue which way Ireland's room was. When we turned down the final hallway, I glanced to her, saying, "I'll pop my head in and get her." Jameson nodded.

"Karen?" I whispered and both she and Ireland looked over to me. "Can you step out here for a moment?"

Ireland was watching me with such hope in her eyes, but she didn't say anything. I hadn't gone into her room since she'd kicked me out, but I made sure she knew I was in the hospital in case she changed her mind. "You want me to come in and sit with you?" I finally asked. She nodded, and I swore, it was the best feeling in the world.

I stepped out just as Karen was snapping a photo with her phone of the paperwork that Jameson held out. "This is great news," Karen exclaimed. "I'm so happy for you and Ireland."

"Thanks, I'm pretty happy too."

"When the nurse came in to check Ireland's vitals, she said the doctor should be by around one. If he lets her go, then you are free to leave with her." It was then, right then, that it hit me. This was really happening.

I was going to be a father, be responsible for someone else.

And as Karen said, at one o'clock the doctor came by and examined Ireland, inspecting her wrist and feeling her head for any soft areas. When he was done, he declared her free to go.

"So, I'm staying at the Double Tree hotel, let's go there and then we can get you some clothes."

"I want to go home. Please, let me go home," Ireland begged. "Besides, I have clothes there."

I had no clue what the right thing to do was. She was wearing kid-size scrubs in a muted, military green. They were ugly, but they were cute on her. So, it wasn't as if she didn't have *anything* to wear out of here, so we could technically go to either place. But, then again, I wasn't all that sure that her being in that house was a great idea.

Would it hurt or help her to be in a familiar space?

If it helped, it would help a lot, but if it hurt, I could always just take her somewhere else. "Yes, we can go to your house. But if you want to leave, just say the word. Okay?"

"Thank you."

We made our way out of the hospital and out to my car. "Are you supposed to have a booster seat or something?"

She gave me a you-are-an-idiot look. "I'm seven, I don't have to sit in a booster seat. Do you see the size of me?"

"Yeah. What's wrong with your size?"

"Sheesh. I'm ginormous. I'm the tallest kid in Sunday school. Jonah, he's ten and in the fifth grade, he was the tallest until we joined the church, now I am."

I held up my hands in surrender, "Okay, no booster seat, I'm sorry."

We got into the car and punched her address into my GPS before pulling out of the parking lot.

"Hey, I need to call my assistant, okay?"

Ireland nodded as she stared out the window.

"Hey, boss, what's up?" Heidi answered.

"You're on speaker, Ireland is here with me. She was released from the hospital."

"Oh, that's so wonderful." Heidi's voice had turned bright, as if she were standing in front of Ireland and smiling down at her.

"Yes, it is. She wants to go to her house, so we are going to head there."

"Is that where you are going to stay the rest of your trip?" Heidi asked.

"I believe so, it's what she wants." I glanced over at Ireland, who was nodding.

"No worries. I'll get it all taken care of and call you back in a few with the details." Heidi hung up, and I drove in silence, Ireland peering out the window, occasionally lifting her unbroken hand to wipe at her cheeks.

When we pulled into the driveway of her house, I didn't know what to expect. I got out and followed her closely. Her head was held high, her back straight, but if it weren't for her fingers, even the ones sticking out from her cast, I'd never know that she was nervous. Her fingers moved as if she were tapping along to a song I couldn't hear. Slowly, I took one of her hands in mine, and she looked up at me and nodded. A silent gesture, she was ready. I unlocked the house and stepped in; Ireland took off running toward a room down a hallway. I assumed it was hers.

AARON

"*H*ey, Heidi."

"Hey, boss, Okay, I called the attorney, Jameson Lane, and got the address of where you'll be staying."

"I could have given that to you."

"You have enough on your plate, besides, you're paying us." I shook my head but was really thankful that she was handing this for me. "I've called the Double Tree and taken care of everything there, they will send all of your belongings out to you."

"Wow."

"Don't be impressed, it cost you."

"Of course it did." No surprise, everything seemed to cost. "I need some recipes and shit, you know, I have to get her food and don't exactly want to go out."

"Already taken care of. I set up with a local restaurant to deliver meals to you. Just keep in touch with me so I know if we need to adjust the times, but right now, I have breakfast and lunch being delivered at seven in the morning and dinner and snacks will be brought by around six."

"I so don't pay you enough," I groaned.

"You do, normally you barely use me, so we can consider this you catching up a little with your two years of overpayments. We're good."

I let out a long, pent-up breath. "I'm worried." I slid my hand through my hair and took a seat, doubting myself for the first time.

"It's going to work out, you are doing what's right, I believe that with my whole heart."

"But I don't have anything at my house for her."

"You have several extra bedrooms that are furnished; they'll be perfect until the two of you can go shopping. It will be a great time to bond, let her choose her decor."

"You're right. Hey, I'll have to call you back, someone's at the door."

"It should be dinner." I glanced at my watch, shocked that it was already six in the evening. "Call if you need anything," Heidi said and disconnected.

I opened the front door, and the kid's eyes in front of me slowly moved up, up, up, taking in my height. "You're . . . you're Aaron Skkye, aren't you?"

"Come on in, what do I owe you?" I led him to the kitchen so he could drop off the banker-style box he was carrying.

"Nothing, it was all paid for including the tip."

"If you promise to keep it quiet, yes, I'm Aaron Skkye."

"I promise. My parents own the restaurant, so I'll be delivering your stuff. Would you mind signing one of your rookie cards if I bring it with me next time I come?"

"Not at all. But, remember, I need you to keep my being here quiet. I'm here for a funeral and would prefer not to have a crowd."

"I'm so sorry for your loss, sir." The kid was more polite than I remember being at his age. "I understand, I won't tell anyone." The kid removed all the takeout cartons from the box and carried the banker file out with him. "See you in the morning."

"Thanks." I felt so guilty for not asking his name.

But before he closed my door, he hollered back, "Hey, someone else is here."

"Crap. I'm not expecting anyone."

"It's some guy," the kid said. "He's in black town car."

"Will you ask him what he needs, for me?"

"Sure, no problem." I listened as the kid stopped the man. "Hi, can I help you?"

"I'm with the Double Tree and have brought Mr. Skkye's things from his room for him."

"I can take those for him. Is there a bill or anything?" the kid asked, all professional.

"No, the bill has been taken care of, and a copy was emailed to his assistant."

"Okay, have a nice evening." The kid headed back toward me, so I opened the door for him.

"You handled that perfectly. I owe you. What's your name?"

"Logan, Logan Greiner."

"Thanks, Logan."

"Any time. I'll see you tomorrow." Logan left, and I opened the boxes to see what was sent over and smiled.

Steak and potatoes. Heidi knew me so well. Then I moved to another large box, which was chicken fingers with french fries and then I opened the last large box, which was spaghetti with meatballs, both were kid-size servings. Quickly opening other foil-wrapped items, I found fresh cookies and all the condiments we would need. Plus, there were several individual-size bags of chips. I shook my head; Heidi was a nurturer.

I just needed to persuade Ireland to join me. Tapping my knuckles a few times on her door, I called out, "Ireland, dinner is here."

"Not hungry," she called back, but her voice was soft and broken. I twisted her doorknob and found the door locked.

"Ireland, please unlock your door. There's spaghetti and chicken fingers with french fries, you can have whichever you want or a little from both. There are also fresh cookies." She still didn't reply. I stretched out on the floor, my body straight out in the hallway since her room was at the end. Resting my chin on one hand, I slid my other under her door and wiggled my fingers. "Ireland, please."

"I want to be alone."

"I understand that."

"No you don't, you had parents, I don't."

"I didn't have a dad."

"Everyone has a dad, it takes a dad to create a baby," Ireland stated, as if I were dumb.

"It takes a man not a dad, a dad is a word that is earned, dad means he loves his child, takes care of them, is there for them. I never had a dad and never knew who the man was that helped create me."

"But you had a mom," Ireland rationalized.

"Yes, I had a mom, but I'm going to tell you something about my mom, something that many people don't know. Your parents knew this, though. My mom was very, very, sick."

"She died too?" Ireland's voice softened, but then I felt a wisp of pressure against my fingers before her fingertips landed on mine.

"No, but when I was little, my mom used to leave me alone for days. I had no way of getting food or even changing myself, I was that little. I'd crawl into our cabinets, but there wasn't anything. So, I'd leave my house, and eventually, someone would call the cops, and I'd get placed into a home with strangers until they found my mom."

"Where was she?"

"Do you know what drugs are?" What age did kids who didn't grow up around them learn about drugs? I felt like I always knew what they were.

"Yes, they're bad for you. They can kill you."

"Yep, but they will also make you think things that aren't true and make you forget things that are important, like that you have a child."

"Your mom forgot she had you?" Ireland's voice was louder, a little more in awe.

"Many times, and when she did, I would get put with a strange family until my mom got some help and I could go back to her."

"Were the families nice?"

"They weren't mean, but they had their own children to take care of, and they were just watching me."

"I'm sorry." Ireland's small hand tightened around a few of my fingers. "Where's your mom now?"

"She's in a place where she can't get drugs. But she doesn't know me, she doesn't know anyone, she doesn't even know who she is. Drugs made her forget everything."

"Do you see her?"

I hadn't seen her since the judge awarded me my emancipation, and I chose to spend my senior year in the apartment above my algebra teacher's home. "No, she wouldn't know who I was. She mostly sleeps all day. I check on her, though, and call the home where she lives and ask about her." I felt Ireland's grasp release, and my heart paled.

The click of the lock had me getting to my knees, but before I was up, Ireland opened her door. "Can I have the spaghetti?"

My soul soared. "You can have whatever you want. We weren't sure what you liked."

"We?" Ireland glanced up.

"Heidi, she is my assistant, she helps with a lot of things."

"Is she your wife?"

I laughed. "No, Heidi is married to someone else and has two sons. They're actually close to your age."

Ireland stopped by the bathroom and washed her hands before heading into the kitchen to grab silverware.

I popped her spaghetti into the microwave and then slid it onto a paper plate that had been sent with the food while my steak and potato heated.

"What smells yummy?" Ireland asked.

"Steak, you want some?"

She nodded. "You can have some of my spaghetti."

"We also have chicken fingers and fries," I reminded her.

"Don't forget the cookies, I have those," Ireland said as she balanced the plate of them in the crook of her arm without a cast on the wrist and brought them to the table.

"Yeah, let's not forget those." I rolled my eyes.

I wanted to pause this moment, take it in, because I knew they would be few and far between for a while. Still, each time she forgets that her tiny world had fallen apart and this man, who was practically a stranger, was trying to push himself in and help her mend it.

Bringing the plates over to the table, I took the seat next to Ireland. "How much steak do you want?"

"All of it." She giggled. "Just a little, my mom says—" She paused for a second and tried to rein it in. "She says that my eyes are bigger than my stomach."

"That's normal when we're hungry," I assured her. "How about I give you this much?" I cut a third of the New York Strip for her and held it up on my fork.

"Yeah, thanks." Ireland's voice had softened again.

"You want me to cut it up for you?"

"Nooo, I can do that." She got up and went to a drawer, then brought back some weird-ass plastic knife.

"What's that?" I asked, pointing to the teal blue cutting object that didn't look like it would cut anything.

"My knife." Ireland sawed into her steak, and it hurt me to watch. Okay, it wasn't the best cut, but still, it didn't need shredding.

"You sure you don't want help?" I asked again.

"Nope, I got it."

We ate in silence, Ireland finally growing tired of cutting and moving on to her spaghetti while I was picking at the chicken nuggets.

"Where are my mom and dad?" Ireland asked while my mouth was full, and I took longer than I needed to chew and swallow.

"They are in heaven."

"Their souls are there, where are they, this?" She poked her body.

"They are at the hospital."

"Are we going to bury them? We don't have a big back-yard. Dad buried my parakeet in the backyard."

"People don't get buried in backyards."

"Then where will they go?"

"They have special places for them called cemeteries, your parents already picked out a place they wanted to be just in case anything ever happened to them."

"I can't pay, I don't have money." Ireland appeared so concerned.

"Don't worry about that, it is all paid for." I paused for a moment, not sure where to take this conversation, so instead I decided to keep my mouth shut and just let her talk.

That night before falling asleep, I sent Viv a text.

ME: I'm so sorry that I haven't had time to talk. My world sort of blew up. But know I'm thinking of you.

~

SUNDAY MORNING, Logan delivered fresh pancakes and bacon at seven on the dot, and he also brought my rookie card.

"You play basketball?" I asked him while he unloaded the food boxes.

"Yep, I'm a guard but not first string."

"Keep at it, what year are you?"

"Sophomore, just got my license."

"Keep practicing but keep studying too. People think that athletes just float through school, but we don't. Well, at least those with half a brain don't. Most of us don't end up being Michael Jordan and can ride on the endorsements for years then end up owning our own NBA team. I got my degree in economics. I figured that, if all else fails, I could be a financial advisor for players."

"Will do, thanks, Mr. Skkye."

"Call me Aaron."

"Thanks, Aaron." I smiled as the kid left and then moved to get Ireland.

Rapping on her door, I waited for a second before turning the knob and walking in. My heart skipped seeing her curled up in a tight little ball. I was shocked at how fast and how strong I felt for this little girl. Shuffling toward the side of her bed, I eased myself down and waited a few seconds before gently tapping her shoulder. "Ireland, breakfast is ready."

"Not hungry," she mumbled and curled in tighter.

"It's pancakes and bacon." I was hoping that made a difference; it sure would have to me when I was a kid. Okay, a lot would have.

She reached up and brushed her hair away from her face. "Bacon?"

"Yeah, there's lots and it's hot." I stood and held out my

hand, hoping she would take it. She didn't, but I didn't take it personally.

After breakfast Ireland was back in her room where she stayed, and I was trying to convince her to come watch a movie when my phone dinged.

KAREN: I'm outside, I needed to do a surprise stop and check on Ireland. Let me in. I didn't want to ring the bell in case she was sleeping.

I TURNED off the ESPN highlight reels before opening the door and letting her in.

"Good morning or almost afternoon. How did last night go?" Karen asked as she dropped her large bag on the table and unbuttoned her hideous coat.

"As expected, I think. Good moments and sad ones, she would ask questions and then cry. Random things would hit her and she was sullen, but then a few minutes later she was talking about something else."

"Where is she now?"

"In her room, I think she finding it to be her safe space."

"Okay, if you'll excuse me, I'll go talk with Ireland." Karen headed off, and I fiddled with my phone.

How long are they going to talk? I pulled up Karen's text she'd sent telling me she was here and then checked the current time and realized only seven minutes had passed, not the three hours I had imagined. I pulled up Angry Birds and destroyed a few before checking my time again. Fuck, only three more minutes had passed.

The sound of Ireland's door opening had me setting my phone down and pushing to my feet to find Karen and Ireland walking toward me.

"Tell Aaron what you want to do," Karen coaxed.

"I want to watch a movie."

"Great, which one," I asked, so happy to have her out here.

"Harry Potter."

"I'll leave you two be, see you tomorrow." Karen showed herself out while Ireland grabbed the remote and flipped through to their Apple TV movies.

VIVIAN

*T*he pop was refreshing as I tilted my head and twisted my neck, rolled my shoulders a few times, and glanced at my phone. I had repeated these steps at least twenty times since Aaron last called.

Forty-eight hours, a vague text, and nothing else.

"Hey, come with me." I smiled up at Everly, who was standing in my doorway. She was a paramedic with Orange County fire department and had been hanging out with me and the girls since . . . well, since Stella declared that we were a gang all those years ago.

"I have an idea, come on." Everly held out one hand and pulled me to my feet. "Go put this on; I grabbed it from Ariel since you two are about the same size."

"Wait? Where are we going?" I stopped and asked.

Everly clapped her hands. "Move it, time is money, go, go, go."

I quickly followed the orders of the drill sergeant, and when I was changed, I stood back in the open doorway of my office. "Please tell me you have me in exercise clothes because we are doing a beer crawl and not something truly heinous like working out."

"Come on." Everly pulled me, and I had no choice but to follow.

The ride to wherever we were going was short. When we arrived, I instantly felt better. "This makes me happy, I love Wall Street, but you know we could have stayed and drank at my bar a lot cheaper."

"Not going to a bar," Everly replied. "Look, there are Lara and Stella." Inwardly, I groaned. If anyone was Stella's equal, it was Army Major Lara Bradford. We'd all hung out several times, and the two of them together usually led us to getting kicked out of more than one bar, but it was fun while it lasted.

"Great, now all we need is Harley, and we will have the speak-before-you-think trio," I warned Everly.

"No, they will behave. We are going to take a vinyasa yoga class."

"A what?" I turned to see Sophie coming up behind us. "This isn't like some tantric shit, is it?" Sophie asked. "I'm not getting all sexy with you lot."

"Sex? Did someone say sex?" Stella asked, coming to a stop next to me.

"Shut up, no, this is a stress relieving yoga, it isn't hot yoga, but it is set in a warm room to help muscles relax. Some of the other girls from the station and I go, and it really helps, especially after the shit we see. I thought it would be great for Viv, she's looking a little piqued here lately." Everly bumped my shoulder and gave me a wink.

I loved my friends, I truly did, but sometimes I just wanted to be able to curl up in a ball with a tub of Ben & Jerry's and feel sorry for myself.

The vinyasa studio was on the second floor and plants surrounded the outside doorway: huge, overgrown taro plants and birds of paradise. "Ah hell no, I'm not walking through those plants, what kind of Florida person puts plants this close to their door that you have to push through to get inside? A stupid one that's who," Sophie said from behind me. "Hasn't anyone told her that snakes like to live in planters? Hell, the crew at Wild Animal Control have to stop by Disney's Polynesian hotel several times a day to check for snakes because people sit along those planters, the same with Animal Kingdom."

"Thank you, Miss Mouseketeer, for that lovely tour, now let's go," Lara said and pushed forward.

"Go like this . . ." Stella pressed her tongue against the roof of her mouth and made a strange clicking sound. "Snakes hate it, it hurts their tiny ears, they'll stay away from you."

"Ha, ha, very funny, snakes don't have ears." Sophie rolled her eyes.

"Yeah, but we all would have laughed loud enough at you that the vibration might have scared them." Sophie leaned forward and kicked Stella in the butt.

"You're such a bitch, but god, I love you."

"It's a talent, what can I say?" Stella flicked a hand in the air as if it was already known by all and then we all went in and were surrounded by more fucking plants.

"Welcome, welcome. Everly, I see you brought some friends. Please remove your shoes and grab a mat. You can find a place anywhere."

I was the first to get moving.

"Look at her go. You've really changed your mind about this yoga, haven't you?" Everly asked.

"Nope. I just figured there was only so much room in the back, so I better be first to grab it so no one ends up making fun of my ass."

That truth was all it took for my entire group to rush to

grab mats and haul ass into the studio, pushing and laughing as they scrambled to grab a spot in the back.

"Excuse me, would you mind moving forward? We're all together," Stella asked some stranger so she could sit in the back too.

The guy next to the woman who had moved, looked at our group. "I guess you'd like me to move as well?"

"You're an absolute doll for offering." Stella smiled, using her Marilyn-Monroe looks to get what we needed.

Katy and Leo scooched close so they could fit in that spot, and Piper ended up next to them.

The cloying smell of patchouli mixed with what smelled like jasmine and cinnamon filled the air. I wasn't sure whether to light up a blunt and go all Cheech and Chong, take a luxurious bath, or get in the flipping kitchen and bake something. Scanning the room, the decor was more African with vases, dried leaves, and woven straw placemats hung on the walls like decorations.

The instructor stepped forward and rang a triangle. "Jambo."

Everly and several others replied, "Jambo."

"Jumbo," Stella and Lara shouted in unison and then looked at each other and cracked up.

"I'm Willow, I've been granted the right to instruct you. For those who are new, Jambo means welcome. I'm happy to have you here." She turned on the radio and the sounds of wind blowing through a field of grass filled the room. Willow spoke in a soft, lulling tone, trying to relax us, but her selected sound had soft bells going off every now and then.

"Are those supposed to be bamboo whistles?" Katy asked. I shrugged, having no clue.

"Let's begin, Kumbhakasana," she called out, and I stared around the room as did most of the rest of my group except for Everly, Sophie, and, to my utter surprise, Lara, who were already moving into whatever position that was. "Remember to inhale as you come into a high plank position."

I followed the others. "Why don't they just call this push-up position?" I asked no one in particular and several people shhhh-ed me.

"What's with the bells? I feel like Quasimodo," Lara moaned. "Hell, I think that I'd prefer John Mayer over this, and I chose a cat in heat over John Mayer on my latest Buzz-Feed quiz."

"Shhh," Willow hushed the entire room, but I knew that she was speaking to us, the non-model students.

The rest of our class kept going while the eight of us pretended to follow along. "Very good, let's move into Ardha Chandrasana, remember to keep your eyes on your hand on the floor then slowly lift your gaze when you feel your chakras are aligned," Willow instructed.

"Another pose?" Stella asked. "I'm already sweating like a whore in church. Can we get some AC in here? And what the fuck is a chakra, I'm a nurse and I'm pretty sure there has to be a medicine to cure it. Can I spread it to Tristan?"

"Quiet back there, please," Willow said softly.

"It's like a half-moon," Everly whispered. I watched her but saw nothing half-moon about it.

Katy and Leo were cracking up and fighting to hide it. "Umm, there's nothing half-moon about this. It's more like the Planter's factory is having open house," Katy said before collapsing on her mat, laughing too hard to stay upright. "We have our very own pppeanuttt man." Katy bubbled with laughter.

"Holy shit," Leo gasped as she tried to stay in this weird triangle position, kicking one leg up.

"What's so funny?" Stella hissed.

"Come see for yourself." Katy gave a head tilt, and like a bunch of rodeo clowns, hopping one over the other, Stella moved into Leo's spot, Leo moved into Katy's, and Katy moved one down into Everly's, who ended up in Stella's place.

Stella stared at the man in front of her and grimaced. "Great hairy balls of China, dude!"

AARON

"*W*here are we going?" Ireland asked, as I fixed my tie.

"We have to go talk to a judge, but don't worry because Miss Karen will be with us."

She nodded while mumbling, "Don't leave me, please."

Kneeling, I wrapped her in my arms and pulled her into a hug. "I will never leave you. I'll be right next to you the entire time. We're meeting with a judge named Martin Cree, do you know him?"

"I think so. I think he's been to the house before." Ireland pinched her eyes as she tried to remember back.

The ride to the courthouse was quiet, and I held her hand as we walked around the building and then was jerked back by the tug from Ireland's hand as she dug her feet in at the base of the courthouse.

"You okay?" I asked.

She studied her shoes. "This is where my dad worked. Do I have to go?"

"I'm sorry, yes. The judge may want to talk with you."

"Why? I don't want to talk to him." Ireland's face was a

mixture of confusion and frustration. "I want to be left alone."

Bending to her height, I placed a hand on each shoulder. "I know you do. You are so brave. We're almost done with all of this and then you and I can decide what we want to do, okay?"

"You promise?" Her lip trembled as though she expected me to tell her anything but what she needed to hear.

With one index finger, I gestured as if to cross my heart while I told her, "I promise."

Jameson was waiting for us as we got to the top of the steps. Since she was my attorney, I knew she had to be ready to play hardball, but I wasn't sure exactly how Jameson interpreted that phrase. I held the door for the ladies to go in and then swallowed down my nerves and followed, Ireland never once letting go of my hand. I had not been in a courthouse since I was sixteen and asked for emancipation from my mother. But it still had the same vibe that felt as if someone was watching you.

After going through the metal detectors, we took the elevators up to the next floor, and Jameson talked the entire way.

"Okay, like I explained before, the judge is going to talk with Karen first and then he will speak with you Aaron. He will want you alone so that he may ask you candid questions." The elevator opened and we headed left down the hall. "Ireland can stay outside with Karen and me. Finally, he'll ask Ireland if she would like to speak to him alone or if she would like you or Karen in chambers with her."

"I want Aaron with me," Ireland interrupted.

"That's fine, honey, you don't have to speak to him alone, it is up to you. Then lastly, we will all be in there together for his final ruling on the case. Then that's it."

"Miss Lane, the judge is ready," an older woman said as

we came to a stop outside his chambers. She held open the door for us, and we all took a deep breath before moving forward.

Judge Cree was younger than I had expected. At most, he was in his late thirties, and he was in shape. He wasn't wearing a black robe, just normal clothes.

"Mr. Martin," Ireland called out and ran to him.

"Hey, sunshine, I'm so sorry. How are you doing? Your wrist looks like it hurts."

"It does, but there's nothing I can do about it."

"Nope, I guess there isn't. Let's all sit so we can get this started." Judge Cree continued to hold Ireland in his lap as he spoke. "This case is personal to me as you can tell. Not only because I care about this little girl but also because I'm the one who drew up all the documents for Ryan and Shannon. They were very clear about what they wanted and explained all the reasons to me. I received all of the documents from Mrs. Koehler at the DCF—"

Karen raised her hand slightly. "That's me."

The judge continued, "Very good. Ireland?"

"Yes?"

"Look at me." Ireland turned so her back was to us. "You can whisper in my ear, I can ask everyone to leave the room, or you can just say it, whatever, it is up to you. Your mom and dad wanted Aaron to take care of you if anything ever happened to them, you know that, right?"

Ireland nodded. "Yeah, 'cause he's my biological father."

"That's right. Is there any reason why you don't want to live with Aaron?"

"No. I want to live with him."

Hearing her say that lifted something in me that I hadn't known had grown so heavy. I had been so scared that she would say no.

"Very well, sunshine. And, Mr. Skkye, I'm to take it that

you have the financial means to care for a second person considering her future such as college, wedding, and other things the girls deem necessary?"

"Yes, I believe that I can afford those." I gave him a grin.

"Then I declare that you, Aaron Edward Skkye, to henceforth be the legal guardian of Ireland Kelly Lacy. Miss Lane, do you have the documents for us to all sign?"

"I do." Jameson slapped them onto the desk. She was as excited as I was.

WHILE STILL DRESSED UP, we headed to Oak Lawn Cemetery. Heidi had arranged a small graveside burial so Ireland could say goodbye to her parents, who had done an amazing job raising her when I couldn't be there for her.

We walked into the office at Oak Lawn and then were directed to the plots and small covered area surrounded by flowers.

I took a moment to examine some of the cards, noting that Heidi had gone above and beyond. There were flowers from Gage and LeeAnn, and there were still more cards and flowers from some of the other guys on my team. I had asked Gage not to tell anyone, so I was guessing it was Coach who told them that someone I had been close to had passed away. Carmen sent flowers from herself, the team, the team mascot lightning bug, the coaches, and the staff, and one of the five arrangements was addressed to Ireland.

"Who are all these flowers for?" Ireland touched the tips of several buds.

"You, they are from people who want you to know that they are thinking of you and are sorry that you had to go through all of this."

"That's nice of them." She plucked a card and read, "From Gage and Ciara. Who is that?"

"Gage is my best friend, and Ciara is his daughter, she's a baby."

"He knows about me?" Ireland's eyes were wide with disbelief.

"Of course, I told you, I always thought about you," I whispered as a man in a suit holding a Bible walked in, followed by three women carrying instruments: two had violins and one had the larger version, a cello, I think it was called.

"Why are they here?" Ireland asked.

"This is a funeral, this is your time to say goodbye to your mom and dad."

"But I don't want to say goodbye. I want to see them."

"They're right there," I pointed to the two caskets.

"Are they inside?" Ireland squeezed my hand tight but kept her focus on the two caskets.

"Yes."

"Can I see them?"

"No sweetie, their souls are already in heaven, so they won't look like your parents." In actuality, it was a closed casket because of the damage their bodies took during the accident. "The good thing about their souls being in heaven is that they can be wherever you are. When you need them, you just have to talk to them."

"I don't believe that. They're dead, they're never coming back to me." Ireland's voice hitched up a few octaves. "They left me, why didn't I go with them?"

I pulled Ireland over to me, wrapped her in a tight hug. "Shhh, it wasn't your time to go. God knew that you had more things to do. You have to grow up still."

"But I have no one, it isn't fair. I belong to no one."

"Hey." I tilted her face back, so her eyes were locked with

mine. "You have me. I belong to you, and you belong to me. We're a package deal now. Consider us a Happy Meal."

"I'm not very happy." Ireland wiped her cheeks.

"Of course you aren't. But one day, when you don't expect it, you will find yourself smiling and laughing and then you'll know we are a Happy Meal."

"But we're only hamburger and fries. We need a drink to be the whole deal." Ireland's simple proclamation hit me like a ton of bricks in a heart-clenching, belly-rumbling way.

Vivian, my little drinker, she was the drink to our complete package. I needed to call her, no, I wanted to call her, hear her soothing voice. Shaking the thought from my head and promising myself to reevaluate my feelings later, I turned my focus back to Ireland, who needed me.

The minister stopped talking, since obviously we weren't listening and were drowning out his speech, but the strings players kept the music flowing.

"Is there anything you would like to say?" the minister asked Ireland.

"Say about what?"

"To your parents?" he clarified.

"My parents aren't in there. They're up in heaven."

"Very well then." He closed his Bible and moved to the back chair.

"Will I be able to go up and see them, like up here to Evansville, since you live in Orlando?"

"Absolutely, we can schedule a trip to come up, we can stay in your house, and you can visit your parents."

Ireland nodded and then straightened herself and walked over to where both caskets were resting on top of brass mechanism bars. "Mom, Dad, I love you. Stay with me, will you come with me to Aaron's house?" She looked over her shoulder toward me. "Do my parents know that I'm going with you?"

"Yeah, they know. Remember, it's what they wanted," I reminded her.

"Oh yeah, how did you know that's what they wanted, did my dad tell you?"

"Your dad left me a letter asking me to take care of you if anything ever happened to them."

"Aww, okay." Her head bobbed as she took that in. "So, I'm going with Aaron, you know him, Dad we used to watch him play . . ." I stared at Ireland as her mouth continued to move, but her words fell so soft that I couldn't make them out. So, I just waited. From what I had read online, patience was going to be the key with her. Sources said that her mood was going to run the entire gamut and sometimes that will be within just the first few hours of waking up.

"Okay, I'm done," Ireland announced, pulling me from my thoughts. "They are going to check in with me in Florida, but they are happy."

A shiver went down my spine. "How do you know this?"

"They told me." She was so firm in her answer.

"You saw them?"

"Sort of." Ireland leaned down. "See those two butterflies on the end of Mom's casket? That's them. Mom always told me to look for butterflies."

Who was I to deny what she said as truth? "Let's go back to your house and pack up whatever we can fit into my car for you to take with us." Ireland wrapped her hand in mine. "If you want all new stuff then we can just buy you new things."

VIVIAN

"*V*ivian, what happened with you and Skkye?" one of the firemen asked. He was a frequent patron at Sixes and had been here the night Aaron came in to see me.

Ever since that night, the Lightning games were often on the television, and tonight was one of those nights.

"Nothing happened, we're still friends."

"I thought you two were more than friends."

"Nope, just friends."

"Why wasn't he playing tonight? Ever since he ran out of Thursday's game, he hasn't played, not once."

"He had a family emergency."

"What the fuck?" Stella grabbed the television remote from the counter and turned up the volume.

Aaron's face was front and center, along with a sweet-looking woman and a child who looked totally like Aaron.

"Celtics beat the Lightning seventy-four to sixty-five in tonight's game without their star shooting guard Aaron Skkye, who hasn't been seen since last Thursday's game. No one has heard word from Skkye's representative or the team's spokespeople as to why he left the game or when he is expected to return. But we may have uncovered something, a sister station in Evansville, Indiana captured this image while covering another story at the Vanderburgh county courthouse. Mr. Skkye was spotted leaving the courthouse with Karen Koehler, a case worker with the county's department of Children and Family Services, and a young child. Keep watching as we continue to follow the mystery of what our golden boy is up to. I'm Haley Loles with Channel Two News."

"What the hell is this, did you know anything about this?" Stella shouted.

"Nope. He told me it was a family emergency, and we're leaving it at that until he tells me otherwise." I hollered back.

"What the fuck is going on?"

"Don't know, don't care."

"Have you spoken to him since he ran out of the game?" Stella's voice softened as she neared me.

"Yep."

"How many times? When?"

"That's two questions." Stella gave me her evil, don't-fuck-with-me-bitch stare. "I talked with him Friday."

"So, you're telling me you haven't talked to him for almost a week? Have you at least tried texting him, relationships even those just beginning are a give and take kind of thing?"

I shook my head.

Stella sighed. "I don't get it, that man is crazy about you, he is dead gone."

"He still might be, but he has a major family issue that he needs to take care of first."

The bell above the door rang, and I turned to welcome the newcomers but froze at the sight of Channel 2 News, Haley Loles along with two men, both carrying cameras with a huge mic.

"We're here to eat, can we sit anywhere?" Haley asked.

"Nope, please leave," I stated, trying to hold my composure. How dare she come into my establishment and try this shit?

She let out a long huff. "We're just here for service."

"Yep, and I'm refusing it. Please leave."

In well-rehearsed movements, the three of them were in position revealing their true reason for being here. "Then let me ask you, Vivian Haines, Orlando's Sweetheart, what is going on with you and Aaron Skkye and is it already over? Does he have a secret love child?"

"That's it," Harley ordered as she removed the mic from Haley's hand. "You were asked to leave, and you've refused. Now, I'm in charge." I smiled as Deputy Harley Scott, a great friend, guided the three of them out and other officers followed behind.

"So, I can take this as you refusing to answer?" Haley shouted back toward me.

"You can take it as you're a bitch," Stella shouted back. "And no one likes you."

"That's it, I'm headed home, Mikki you've got this?" I asked.

"Absolutely, go home and chill. We'll be fine," she assured me.

"Nope. We're not having that." Stella tugged my hand. "Danny, can I have a shaker, some limes, and a bottle of Patron?"

"Coming right up," Danny shouted back as he grabbed a bowl of sliced limes and began filling a tray.

"That"—I pointed toward the door—"is just one more reason why Aaron and I would never work, I hate the media."

"Yep, don't we all." Stella was placating me as she pulled me to the corner table.

We all sat while Danny delivered a stack of shot glasses, tequila, limes, and several salt shakers.

Everly, who had been sitting with some of the firemen and paramedics, joined us and began filling glasses.

"Take a lime and shake your salt," Stella said as she shook her ass for emphasis.

I held up my glass and announced, "Haley is a bitch." We all slammed our first shot back.

Everly immediately began refilling while the rest of us grabbed our lime and salt.

"Men are assholes," I proclaimed as I waved my glass in the air again, and everyone downed their second shot. "I feel like we need some J-Lo and Shakira in here."

Sadie, one of the deputies, ran to the jukebox and searched for songs. When "Booty" came on, we all got into the rhythm and got two—or maybe five—more shots into us as well.

By the time we had listened to every Latin artist we could think of and I believed that I could now speak Spanish, my world was spinning. Not as in spinning out of control but spinning as in, the fucking room wouldn't stop moving.

"Okay, pile into my car, I'll take you all home," Everly announced.

"Hey." I patted her cheek. Everly grabbed my hand. Okay, maybe I patted a little too hard. "You can't drive and drink." I thought about what I had just said. "Um, I mean drink and drive."

"I haven't had a drink; I've been filling the glasses and watching you be crazy-ass fools."

"No." I shook my head, which made my stomach shake too. "Not crazy-ass fools, crazy over some asshole."

"Night," I hollered to everyone in Everly's car.

"Night, sweetie," Sadie called after me.

"Love you, bitch," Stella boomed for my neighbors' listening pleasure.

"There's no crying in baseball," Harley shouted.

"What?" I turned around and almost stumbled. "What?" I asked again.

"I don't know. It sounded good to me when I said it."

I paused and stared at Harley like the freak she could be. "You're weird."

"Nah, just drunk."

I unlocked my door and stepped in, letting out a sigh of relief at finally being home. For some reason, I wanted to talk to Aaron, like now. I needed to hear his voice and tell him exactly how I felt.

Stumbling back to my bedroom while dialing him on the phone, I decided that I could multitask. I'd get ready for bed and talk.

"Hello?"

I paused for a second, waiting for the beep.

"Vivian?"

I slipped on my nightgown and then crawled onto my bed. "Aaron?"

A chuckle rang through my phone. "Yes, you called me."

"Oh, I thought I would get your voicemail or something. I was wondering why it didn't have a beep. Your voicemail does have a beep, doesn't it? I have to ask because I don't think I've ever left you a message before."

"I think I have a beep, I've never called myself before. But enough about the beep, it's good to hear your voice."

"You hurt me. No, that isn't it, you pissed me off. I was starting to like you, but you blew it. Vivian Leigh Haines does not give second chances."

"Oh. I hate to hear that because while you may have been just starting to like me, I was starting to more than like you."

"But you left me. I know you had an emergency, and I

shouldn't be upset because being upset when someone has an emergency is kind of a dick thing, but then it was nothing, nada, nothing but a text, that was all." I leaned back and rested my head against the headboard. "Men kinda suck, you know? Or maybe it's me. I can't figure it out. I hadn't let anyone in, not even an inch, since Eric died, and the first person I do is not for me. How fucked up is that, like really? You left me there to face that Haley-bitchface-Loles. She kept shoving a mic and camera in my face to see if I was the person you were smiling at and asking why you left. I hate the media, have I ever told you how much I hate the media?"

"No, why do you hate them?"

"They are bottom feeders. They think everyone's business is their business. They forgot the basic human respect that there are times you need to leave people alone, like when you are trying to bury someone. They want to exploit your every emotion and reaction as if it is everyone's business how you cry or when you rage against things that are happening. It's messed up, seriously messed up."

"Yeah, I agree. They are intrusive. I don't mind when they ask about plays after a game, but when I'm not on the court, I'm a normal person. For the most part, they let me be a normal person. I would rather them interview a doctor and ask them how many lives they saved today, or a judge and ask how many dangerous criminals they got off the streets." Aaron's voice was like perfectly aged brandy, mellow, smooth, and hung in the air with languid notes.

"How about not even them? Politicians only. If you run for a public position, then you are offering yourself up to public opinion. Then I wouldn't have to deal with crap like Haley Loles coming into my bar to bombard me with questions."

"She showed up at your work? What happened? You okay?"

"Nothing." I scoffed. "She shouted a bunch of questions, but you know my patrons. They weren't putting up with her shit. But, yeah, I'm fine. Oh wait, do you have a secret family?"

"What?" He chuckled. "No, I don't have a secret family."

"No. Stop. Don't lie to me." Okay, I was two sheets to the wind, but even I could tell I sounded like a whiney-ass woman. "I saw some pictures. You were with a woman and a girl; the girl looks just like you."

"Some people that I had a very close bond to were killed in a car accident, which is why I had to leave immediately. The woman in that picture was the case worker. There's so much more I want to explain, but would you mind if we talked about it tomorrow . . . when you will remember?"

I should have been annoyed that he thought I was too drunk to remember, but his voice was warm and soothing, as if he were smiling through the words.

I liked it, but I also hated that he had lost people he was close to.

"Viv?"

A heavy sullenness had settled over me, making it hard to talk. "Yes? I'm sorry about your friends."

"Thank you. Grab some water and drink a lot before you go to sleep. But, trust me, I really want to see where we can go. I'm leaving tomorrow, okay. Good night, my midnight call girl."

"Night, Aaron." I disconnected and dropped my phone.

AARON

She's a girl, one hundred percent female.

I glanced back at Ireland, who was seated in my backseat in the most uncomfortable position possible. Her face rested on the strap of the seatbelt that was strung across her chest, which forced her head to tilt in a weird way. My neck hurt just watching her.

Toys were stacked and crammed into every nook and cranny around her in the tiny backseat of my Porsche Cayenne. The girl had no problem agreeing to all new clothes and shoes but absolutely refused to leave any of her toys.

Kids.

Once we'd taken care of what we could at her parents' house, we got on the road. I had no idea how many hours having a kid in the car would add to a road trip. I think that I made a total of twelve stops for a twelve-hour trip, we ate at restaurants not fast food because that was what she wanted, and I would bet that Ireland saw the inside of every bathroom stall between Evansville and Orlando. The kid either had a tiny bladder or a freakish curiosity for toilets.

"Hey, boo, we're here," I whispered as I shut the garage door. "Wake up, let's go inside." I turned off the ignition, got out, and opened the house before returning and helping a sleepy Ireland out of the car. How she was sleepy was beyond me, since if she wasn't hungry or in need of a restroom, she was asleep. "We'll unpack your stuff tomorrow, let's just go in, and you can go to bed."

"But where?" Ireland grunted and yawned at the same time.

"I have five guest rooms, you can have whichever one you want." That seemed to perk her up.

"Where's your room?" she asked as we walked into the kitchen.

"Mine is right over there." I pointed to the oversized double doors at the far end of the hallway. "The other rooms are down over there." I pointed to the two side wings of the house. "You can choose any one you want."

Ireland shuffled off to look and explore. I plopped down on the sofa and picked up the remote.

Flipping through channels, I paused when Ireland shouted, "Can I have this one?"

I followed her voice and found her in a spacious room. It was beige—okay, my entire house was beige, but still, this one lacked all color.

She was already up in the bed and had her shoes off.

"You can have whatever you want, you ready for bed?" I reached into her backpack that she had set by the door and pulled out her pajamas.

"I'm tired." Her words were soft, and I couldn't tell whether it was from sleep or sadness creeping in.

"Okay, get changed and brush your teeth. Tomorrow, we can make a list of everything you need and do some shopping if you want?"

"Yeah, okay," she mumbled as she grabbed her bag and PJs, then headed toward the bathroom.

"There are new toothbrushes and some toothpaste in the drawer in there." Okay, I wasn't sure which drawer, but I knew they were there since my housekeeper kept it stocked with all the normal toiletries just in case some of the players crashed here. As I thought about that, I rushed to the nightstand and jerked the drawer open. Before Ireland had a chance to find them, I removed the unopened box of condoms that were also kept in each room. That's the second I realized a lot of things were over for me, and for some reason, I wasn't sad. It was almost a relief, as if I had done my part and I could move on to what I really wanted to do.

A few minutes later Ireland came back out dressed for bed. She climbed under the covers, and I moved to sit next to her. Gently brushing her hair back, I lowered a soft kiss to her forehead. "I know this is hard and that everything hurts so much, but we're going to get through this together. You and me, okay?"

"Okay." She rolled over onto her stomach and turned her head away from me, a silent gesture that said so much. She wanted to be left alone.

Turning off the lights, I stood there for several seconds. "I love you."

As I headed back out to the living room, an emptiness washed over me, and I found myself reaching for my phone. It wasn't even ten yet, so she was still awake.

VIVIAN

"Hello?" I answered even though I wasn't sure how much I was willing to hear him out.

"Hey, Little One, I just got home, and I was wondering if you wanted to come over."

"It's late, if you just got home go to bed, we can talk tomorrow," I assured him, keeping my heart guarded.

"It isn't that late, plus there is so much I want to talk to you about. What if I said please?"

The pleading in his voice changed something in me. Aaron was all man, but the softness in his tone had me giving in.

"Where do you live?" I asked, more resigned, and wrote down the Bayhill address as he rattled it off. "I'll see you in about twenty-five minutes."

I hung up and then quickly gathered my things from my office before waving goodbye to Danny and Mikki.

With the window rolled down, the cool night air blowing through my hair, and Billy Joel crooning "The River of Dreams," I headed west toward the Bayhill area. I had no clue what to expect when I got there, I'd been racking my brain, trying to figure out what was so important that he couldn't tell me what it was over the phone. It was like some riddle, but of course, my mind went to the extremes, like he was married and wanted me to meet her. Okay, I was being ridiculous, but I was baffled. I exited the interstate and turned onto Sand Lake Road just as my GPS was saying to exit now.

"Nice try, dipshit, you're a little late," I said to the robotic woman's voice.

When I pulled up to the guard gate, I handed my license over and was immediately waved through. Aha, at least he alerted them that I was coming. When I pulled into his driveway, the first thing that dawned on me was that Sixes and my house could fit inside his home. Good god, what did a single guy need with a house this big? Okay, no one *needed* a house this big, unless we were talking about the *Brady Bunch* or Octomom.

I turned off my car and then just sat in his driveway, constantly checking my rearview and side mirrors. Maybe I expected whatever his secret was to jump out at me. When nothing did, I sighed and opened my door. I turned to walk up to his front door and found him standing on his porch, a wide smile on his face. Okay, that was reassuring, at least. How bad could this be if he was happy?

I headed up to him and then was engulfed by everything that was Aaron Skkye, his height, his cologne, his sheer strength.

"You feel so good, thank you for coming out," he whispered before stepping back, locking eyes with me.

"Well, only the best secrets are worth a drive in the middle of the night to hear." I was grinning because my nerves had settled, and the heaviness of trepidation had lifted. Then he was kissing the smile away, drinking me in as if he couldn't get enough. "God, Vivian, I can't tell you how good it feels to have you here."

"It feels nice being in your arms."

"Come on, let's go inside."

Beige, the place was beige, which was the only sense that I had of his home, lots of beige walls, ecru window treatments, and walnut-colored accents. I never wanted to give a kid a box of crayons and tell them to brighten the place up more than I did the moment I stepped into Aaron's some-several-million-dollar home.

"I have some red wine out already for you." Aaron pulled me over to a deep, plush, dark brown couch and sat. "How are you? You look beautiful, and I can't believe how much I missed our chats."

"I missed you too." I took the glass of wine that Aaron handed me and slowly sipped, watching him over the rim of my glass. I relaxed with my glass and Aaron reached for it, setting both of ours back on the table before he grasped my hands.

"I had a bad childhood, there's no other way to say it. From as early as I could remember my mom would leave me and go off on some drug bender. It would be days before I saw her again. There were many times she left and there was no food, so I did what anyone would do: I went looking."

My heart froze, because what kind of mother could leave a child? My god, this meant he was what, three or four?

"Sometimes the police would find me and take me to a foster home, but other times I would find my way back and wait for her to come home. I'm not telling you this to feel sorry for me; I can see it on your face. I'm telling you so that you understand me."

"Okay." I bit my lower lip to keep from saying anything else.

"My life was spent being jostled around from my mom to

foster homes and back to my mom. I don't think that I ever felt love until my first real girlfriend. She would tell me that she loved me, and it was such a strange feeling, but I liked it. Her name was Maisy."

He reached forward and swept a stray strand of hair off my cheek. "She was the first girl I had sex with."

Hearing about him having sex with someone else bothered me, it was weird, it shouldn't, because it was a long time ago, but still.

"Uh, Aaron, you don't need to tell me all of this. It's okay, really."

"But I do. Maisy got pregnant. At first, she wanted to have an abortion, and I wanted to keep the baby. I wanted to be different, show a child the love I never got. I thought she had changed her mind, and she was coming to see things my way. But shortly after delivery, when they wheeled the baby off so Maisy could sleep, she got up and snuck out of the hospital. No one has seen or heard from her since."

I gasped. "What? She just left?"

"Yep, vanished. I had this whole life imagined. I was going to negotiate housing so my family, meaning Maisy and our daughter, could come with me. I would work and play. She could go to school and watch our daughter, when she had class, we could take advantage of the childcare center on campus. I had imagined this perfect world that I hadn't had. But she left and it left me as a sixteen-year-old single dad."

"Oh my god, what did you do? Where is the baby now?"

Aaron gave a wry smile. "I was already being scouted by colleges—"

"But you were sixteen, that's what, tenth grade? You still had two more years."

"I was in eleventh, but my point is that I knew it wasn't the best situation or time for me to take care of a baby, she—"

"It was a girl?" Aaron smiled brightly at me and nodded.

"Yep, a girl. I decided at that time adoption was the best option." I raised one brow, curious about where he was headed. "On the night of the game, Carmen told me that Ireland, that's her name, by the way, and her parents were in a car accident. Her parents were killed on impact."

"She was okay, right?"

"Yeah, a broken wrist and some bumps and bruises, but she'll be okay. The shocker was that when I walked into her room, she knew me; she knew who I was to her, her parents had been open with her and she and her dad would watch me play. I had no clue."

"Awww, poor baby."

"Yeah, it is sad, everything she has gone through."

"If she was adopted, how did someone know to contact you?"

"Ryan Lacy, her adoptive dad, listed me as a contact for Ireland should something ever happen to them. They also stipulated that I regain custody of Ireland if something were to happen to them."

"Mom?" I jumped at the sound of a little girl's voice. Tiny feet were smacking against the tile floor, and I turned just as a dark-haired little girl came to a halt in front of me. "You're not my mom," she cried and then huge wracking sobs broke free and a torrential downfall of tears fell from her eyes.

I reached out for her hand. "No, I'm not your mom, sweetie. But come here, let me hold you." I opened my arms and was shocked as the little girl, who I assumed was Ireland, climbed into my lap.

She was tall and lanky, so much like Aaron that it almost took my breath away.

"Vivian, this is Ireland, my biological daughter," Aaron announced.

I processed his words as I finger-combed her hair and held her close. Oh, what she had been through broke my heart. When I lost my husband, it was earth shattering, but to be a child and lose both parents, it was unconceivable to me.

"Hello, Ireland, I'm Vivian. You're so beautiful."

"Thank you," Ireland whispered but didn't release her hold on me.

"Aaron was just telling me all about you." She tilted her head and stared over to him. Slowly, her tears stopped, but she was still trembling with sadness.

"My mom had black hair just like yours."

"Oh." What else could I say that wouldn't send her back into gut-wrenching sobs?

I sat there for what felt like hours, seeing what could only be described as love radiating from Aaron as he looked over at Ireland.

"Shhh, she's asleep."

He moved closer. "Let me take her."

"No, she's fine."

He nodded slowly and dragged one hand down his face. "As you can see, I gained custody of Ireland. She's going to live with me, and we'll be a family."

"I admire you," I admitted. "I think you are going to be a wonderful dad. She is awful lucky."

"Thanks. But what about you? There's no denying that there is something between us, but I want to know that you're okay with me being a single dad."

"That doesn't bother me at all. I would have been sad if you had told me that story and then didn't have this precious girl. I meant what I said, I admire you." I gazed at Ireland sleeping. "She looks so much like you. I think that she's going to be a basketball player as well."

He grinned, but then we both sat in silence. I hummed to Ireland, my maternal instincts coming out strong. I had always wanted kids—hell, Eric and I had planned on having kids. If my life hadn't gone completely sideways, then I would have had kids years ago.

I wasn't sure when I fell asleep, or how long I'd been asleep, but I processed Ireland being slid out of my arms. I instantly missed her body heat, but at the same moment, it gave me freedom to relax and I was diving back into the pool of dreams.

"Put your arms around my neck," Aaron whispered. It was a strange dream, but I did as he asked. Then I was floating like a feather, and that was when it dawned on me that I wasn't dreaming, this was really happening.

I opened my eyes and lifted my head from his shoulder, but he dropped a soft kiss to my lips to stop the words I was going to say.

"You can stay the night here."

"No, I really should—"

"You really should," he whispered, as he lowered me onto the world's softest bed. It was like a pillow of clouds.

I was already falling back into peaceful sleep by the time he slipped off my shoes and then moved to unbuckle my jeans. Before I knew it, I was in just my T-shirt and panties. He pulled back the covers and tucked me in.

"I'll be in the room next to Ireland, okay?"

"Kiss me," I begged.

He lowered his mouth to mine; the lips that I had missed for a week were on me . . .

VIVIAN

*T*hat felt nice.

I slid my face against the silkiest sheets that smelled like soap and leather as it slowly started to come together. Aaron was kissing me around my neck and along the curve of my shoulders. This wasn't a dream.

"Wait, don't go." Strong masculine fingers wove through mine.

Pulling myself out of my sleep haze, I woke just as he, flipped me to face him, and then leaned in, and lifted me to him halfway. This time I was ready for his kiss, his slightly soft lips that swept back and forth along mine, before I opened and he slid his tongue in.

I was hit with the memory of the first time Eric had kissed me. It had been so passionate we knew it was going to take us to that next level. Kissing Aaron wasn't something that made me feel guilty. After all these years, I thought I would have these gilded chains wrapped around me, but I didn't; I actually felt free. Something about this man, this moment, seemed right.

Aaron leaned up. "Are you—"

"Shhh, don't stop," I begged, digging my fingers into his thick, wavy hair and pulling his face back down to mine. I didn't want our kiss to end. I wasn't ready for this moment to end.

My body jostled as he brought one knee up and rested it on the bed. He deepened our kiss, forcing me back. When he stopped, I was startled, my eyes searching his to see if he'd changed his mind or if I had done something wrong. But all I saw was passion and . . . love.

He clasped our hands together and kissed my fingers. "Are you sure, Little One? If this is too soon . . ."

I shook my head. "I want this, Aaron. I want you. I want this, please . . ." I paused for a second, I was going to say *make love,* but that was presumptuous, since I wasn't sure he felt love for me. But saying fuck me, seemed a little brash. "I need to feel you inside me." There, that was a nice middle ground.

"Gladly." Aaron moved my hands up and released his hold, resting them around his neck. Then he swiftly slid his entire frame next to mine. "You are so beautiful. How did I get so lucky?"

Lucky? Him? He had no clue who the lucky one truly was, he had everything—a sexy body, looks, money, beautiful women throwing themselves at him. He was a star shining bright for everyone, and I was a teeny tiny dust mote, floating through the air unnoticed.

My mind was all over the place, but Aaron was focused, his pressure against my lips increased, and he let out a groan that rumbled straight to my center. His voice rolled down my spine, and I squirmed and tightened my legs in anticipation for him.

Leaning up a few inches, Aaron grabbed his shirt by the collar and pulled it up and over his head before tossing it to the floor. Then his huge hands were tugging my shirt up, but he paused when my bra-covered breasts were exposed.

I was heaving, my body trying to convey what I wasn't saying, and that was that I wanted him—not in a few minutes or even seconds—but right that moment. Thank god, he got the clue, he reached behind me, and faster than any woman could, he unfastened my bra before lowering his mouth to my nipple and sucking.

He kneaded one breast while he sucked on the other only to change positions and continue his assault. When he lifted his hands, it was to remove my shirt and toss it to the slowly growing pile of clothes. I couldn't take my eyes off of his, their swirling shades of brown that only seemed to darken.

Aaron threw his jeans off and then shifted to rest on one elbow. With a groan that sounded more like him trying to control himself than actually enjoying this. He brushed his knuckles along my hip before grabbing on to the side of my panties and peppering kisses down the valley of my breasts and down my torso. His motions were smooth, and as the panties went down, so did his kisses.

"I've never thought of a belly button as sexy before," he murmured with a chuckle. "But yours is. There isn't one inch of your body that doesn't turn me on."

Oh, he had no idea . . .

"Aaron, I want you now. Please, don't torture me any longer," I begged.

Grinning, Aaron flung my panties off the side of the bed and then he was wiggling out of his boxer briefs. He positioned himself over me, and my breathing became rapid and choppy. I grasped hold of his biceps, but he wiggled free and moved his hands to my thighs, gently pushing them open, "So fucking beautiful." Lowering himself to the bed, he moved his shoulders between my legs, and in one long lick, he had me nearly flipping off the bed.

"Holy shit!" I practically yelled.

Aaron only chuckled, his sound muffled because his head

was buried in my pussy, raising one hand, he pressed it to my chest, guiding me back down.

His licks and sucks became more fervent as I lost myself in what he was doing to my body.

The need for release pooled in my stomach, my hips thrust, wanting him to take me over that edge. Aaron pushed me higher and higher. My moans were ripped from me as I was moved closer to orgasm and then I was all but convulsing as he took me over that precipice, and all of my insecurities seemed to melt away.

Before I knew it, he reached for the nightstand to grab a foil wrapper. I followed his movements and for the first time got a good glimpse at his cock. Gasping, I sat up. "Holy fuck, Aaron. How do you tote that thing around?"

He laughed as he rolled the condom down his long, wide, throbbing dick. "Since I met you, it's definitely been a lot *harder* to walk around with." He grinned, obviously amused. But something about that made him look boy-next-door handsome and all man at the same time.

There were no more words or joking, Aaron lowered his lips to mine and something about his kiss. This kiss was different than the others, this one screamed of posses-siveness.

"You're mine now, Little One, all mine. No more excuses, it is us. You're mine."

Aaron finally released my lips and slid up, his fists pressing deep into the mattress on either side of my head as he positioned himself.

He rubbed his cock up and down against me. "So fucking wet," he murmured.

Shivers rippled down me as my fingers dug into his skin. I couldn't believe we were going to do this. I was tense, and I knew it, but I didn't have a clue how to relax, silly fears rummaged in my head.

"Hey," Aaron said softly. "Don't overthink it, Little One. I'll go slowly. Trust me to take care of you."

It was almost a little scary, the way he could read me. Still, it eased my tension, and slowly, I slid my legs wider.

I felt the tip of him poised at my opening and then he slowly glided in. "Maybe I was wrong." Aaron panted, the effort to hold back clear in his strained voice and expression. "Maybe a cherry can grow back."

I burst out laughing and then he pushed the rest of the way in. Aaron sighed, clearly relieved that I had relaxed, and he was seated to the hilt.

"All right?" he asked.

I nodded. "I'm good. I need you to move though."

Aaron slid out and then back in, increasing his pace. The sensations bombarded me, and once again, I found myself spiraling up with each thrust.

Small moans escaped Aaron's lips as he fucked me, his pace a driving force that demanded I give in to what he wanted. Each movement was harder and faster than the one before, and before I knew it, I was there; he had pushed me to the edge and then we were both falling.

VIVIAN

"*R*ise and shine, Ireland and I made breakfast," Aaron called from the bedroom door.

"What time is it?" I groaned as I tossed a pillow over my face.

"Almost nine."

I waited until the door clicked and then sat up. I was at Aaron's, I brought no clean clothes, and Ireland knew that I'd spent the night. Um, this was not okay. Glancing around the beige room, I had to laugh, I was officially in the black hole of boring. God, I could imagine some hunter green and gold accents in here.

I froze.

What the hell was I doing? This wasn't my house, and I had no business mentally redecorating it.

Tossing on what I had worn yesterday, I headed into his bathroom and smiled when I found a wrapped toothbrush, toothpaste, and dental floss on the counter for me. The man really was thoughtful.

Fewer than ten minutes later, I joined Ireland and Aaron

just as Aaron tossed a chocolate chip for Ireland to catch in her mouth.

"Hey, I want one!" I grinned.

Aaron smirked and then had a silent conversation with Ireland using only their eyes. She moved closer to Aaron, they both took aim and then launched chocolate chips at me.

Oh hell no, I was a pro, and there was no wasting chocolate if I was around. I opened my mouth, bent, jerked to the left, and caught the first chip. Then, without wasting a beat, I jumped and caught the second.

"Boom, she scores," I held up my hands and jogged around the kitchen island. That was until several morsels hit the back of my head. "Hey, no wasting chocolate, how many times do I have to tell you?" I couldn't be mad because Aaron and Ireland were laughing. "So, where is this breakfast I heard so much about?"

"Here." Ireland opened the oven door. "We've had the food on warm, you ready to eat?" Aaron reached around Ireland and brought out two pans. "We have pancakes and bacon."

"I'm starved. Who did the cooking?" I asked as I moved to grab plates.

"I did," Ireland said happily. Aaron let out a small cough. "Okay, Dad—" She froze. "I mean, Aaron helped a little." Her tone had changed, and it wasn't as jovial as it had been.

But Aaron was a nurturer. It was strange seeing him as this father figure when I had been comparing him to a college frat boy and me to the older, wiser woman. I was so narrow-minded to think he was anything short of spectacular.

Shoving one hand through my hair, I tried to clear my thoughts and jumped in to help.

"Yummm," I said as I took my first bite. "You're a good

cook, Ireland, you'll need to show Aaron how." Ireland laughed. "What kind of things do you like?"

"I don't know."

"Is cooking something you want to do when you grow up?" I asked, trying to get the little girl to open up to me.

"Maybe."

"I own a small restaurant." Okay, a bar with grille food, but I wasn't going to say 'bar' to her.

"You like cooking too?" Ireland asked as we all moved to the barstools around the island.

"I do, but I don't cook there. I have to do all the book-work and handle the money."

"Can I come see it sometime?" she asked around a mouthful of pancakes.

I glanced up at Aaron for confirmation, "Absolutely."

"Ireland and I were talking about doing some shopping today; you want to come with us?" There was hope in Aaron's eyes as he asked.

"Please, Aaron is a boy, and boys don't shop great." Ireland didn't meet my eyes when she asked it. I wasn't sure if she was asking out of kindness or if she genuinely wanted me to go.

"I'd love to if you really want me to tag along," I agreed. "What all do you need?"

"Everything." Ireland looked up for the first time, and our eyes locked.

"Oh. Okay." Everything? She didn't bring anything from home?

Ireland glanced over to Aaron, and he patted her hand.

"So, you need everything, does that mean clothes?"

"Yes, I brought a backpack full. Aaron's having the rest of my stuff brought here, but it will be a week. Besides, he said I could have all new stuff, so I want new stuff."

I giggled. "Don't blame you there. It's much more fun

when you are spending someone else's money. Do you need anything besides clothes?"

"We were deciding about her bedroom, she needs furniture and stuff for in there," Aaron answered.

"Please tell me that the walls aren't beige, and if they are, can we paint them?" I practically begged.

"They're beige and yucky," Ireland agreed.

"You can paint. You can do anything you want in there," Aaron informed us.

I was getting excited about the project because I loved decorating and painting. "I can paint and draw. I have a friend who has three daughters and I painted big murals on their walls."

"What's a mural?" Ireland was totally interested.

"It's a big picture that you paint on a wall," I tried to explain.

"What did you paint?" Ireland had finished eating.

"In the baby's room, I did the kingdom with the castle from *Beauty and the Beast*, in Gianna's room I did the mine and woods from *Snow White* and then in Harlow's room I did Cinderella's castle."

"Can I have mermaids?" Ireland asked nonchalantly.

"Absolutely. I could paint one wall to look like the ocean with fish, coral, and some mermaids. Then the rest of the walls we can paint another color to match."

"Really?" Ireland pulled her legs up on the stool, so she was sitting in a crisscross position as she looked between Aaron and me.

"Sounds good to me, I told you that it was your room. We just need to know where to go." Aaron grabbed hold of my hand and squeezed.

"Let's make a list. Aaron, do you have paper and pen?" My mind was already whirling with ideas. "Okay, I think we need to start with the important stuff."

"Like clothes?" Ireland asked.

"Yep, and then we can order furniture because that will take several days. After that, we can pick out paint colors you like."

"I'll have to sneak away for about an hour around one o'clock for a meeting. You two can come and sit in the lobby at the arena or keep shopping, and I'll come right back there when I'm done."

I looked over at Ireland and could tell that, while she wanted to go shopping, she wasn't sure about hanging out with me without Aaron around.

"How about we decide after we eat? Let's see how we feel then, okay?"

I glanced at Aaron, who winked at me, and Ireland was relieved.

"Hey, ladies, we have gotten a lot accomplished so far." He held up several bags. "But it's almost one. I have to head to the arena. Do you want to stay and shop or come with me?"

It was the subtle movement, Ireland taking one step closer to Aaron. I knew what I needed to do for her comfort. "We'll go with you. That will give us time to mark off the things we got and decide what we still need."

We piled into the Porsche Cayenne and headed to the arena.

"Can we walk around?" Ireland asked.

"Sure, just stay with Vivian. I'll text you two when I'm done if you aren't in the lobby," Aaron said as we walked around to the side entrance.

A camera flashed, I flinched. "Aaron, where have you been?" a reporter asked.

"Don't you have a home; are you just lying in wait?" Aaron barked back.

"This is my home, and I've been waiting for you."

We ignored him, Aaron didn't say anything else as the

man continued shouting questions and we pushed inside. Aaron locked the door behind him.

"What was that man screaming about?" Ireland asked.

"I'll explain after my meeting, but let me show you where I'll be." Aaron led us down a hall. "See the basketballs on the floor that's what you're going to follow. There are a few halls that look exactly the same, and they put these on the floor so us jock-heads don't get confused." He smiled.

The hallway opened to a lobby that looked to house several offices as well as a giant conference room. "Okay, we've got it from here, right, Ireland?"

"Right." Ireland kept her eyes on Aaron as he stared at her.

"After this, why don't we go get you a cell phone?"

"My very own?"

"Yeah," he said softly. "That way you'll always be able to reach me, okay?"

Her lips were tight, but she nodded.

Aaron headed into the office, and I held out my hand for Ireland, but she didn't take it. So, we just walked side by side. "Do you play basketball?"

"I used to with my dad. Do you?"

"Never played. If you promise not to make fun of me, I'll tell you a secret."

The grin she gave me was wide and full of anticipation. "Promise."

"I don't know how to play."

Her jaw dropped with shock. "You don't know how?"

"Nope. I saw Aaron play once, but that was about it."

"I think that I've seen just about every one of his games."

"You'll have to teach me how to play sometime."

"I can do that. Aaron can help too." Ireland's face lit up with excitement.

We rounded a corner and got our first glimpse of the

court, the same one from the game a few weeks ago. Banners were lining the arena, benches decorated, and a big score-board in one corner.

"Come on." I raced forward, happy that she followed. "This is where Aaron plays when he has home games. I think this might be where he practices too."

"Look." Ireland pointed to a ball. "I'll teach you now." She raced over, grabbed it, and started to dribble. "Catch." She tossed it to me. "Now you dribble." Ireland mimicked bouncing the ball with her hand.

So, I dribbled. I didn't tell her that I knew some simple basics like the word dribble; she was alive with excitement teaching me. I bounced the ball with my left hand, then my right. "Catch." I tossed it back to her.

"Okay, so that's pretty much all we do as we work our way down the court until we get close enough to the basket. Then we shoot. We want the ball to go into the basket."

"Way up there?"

"Yep, way up there."

"Okay. That seems easy enough."

She laughed and passed the ball back to me. I took a step and dribbled, my hand-eye coordination was seriously lacking. Step, dribble, pass—crap, I forgot to shout catch. I watched Ireland as she dribbled and ran at the same time. Her hands moved in sync, and less than a second later, the ball was back to me. Shit, shit, shit. Walk, dribble, walk, dribble. "Catch!"

Ireland giggled as she continued her fluid motions, and we were at the basket. She tossed and missed. "Now your try, Vivian."

I took the ball and focused on the basket. Then I cradled that orange, grainy sphere in both hands, swung almost to the floor between my feet, and launched it toward the basket. It went up, up, and over the basket.

Ireland was on the floor cracking up. "No one shoots like that."

"I do, I just did."

"No, let me show you." She chased down the ball and then moved to stand next to me. "Put one foot forward. Take the ball and hold it up, keep your eyes on the basket. You want to flick your wrist and let the ball smoothly fly. Okay, try."

I followed her instructions and flipped my wrist, but the ball didn't go five feet.

"Maybe we should work on shooting first."

"Really? You think that's all I need work on?" I asked her teasingly.

"Well . . . no. But I didn't want to hurt your feelings."

"Get out of here." We both turned at Aaron's booming voice. I saw the same guy who had been screaming questions at us outside. Out of instinct, I put myself between the stranger and Ireland until Aaron could reach us.

Aaron was racing toward us, shouting even louder, "Security."

The man curved his camera around and was snapping photos of Aaron, who swatted the camera out of his face.

Two men in security uniforms came running downstairs from upper-level rooms. Several people came in from the same direction Aaron had. Ireland took off and rushed to Aaron's side. Pretty soon, there were at least fifteen people huddled around Aaron and the photographer.

I stood there, watching from the peripheral of the group. One minute passed, then two, then five, and still no one turned to see me, they moved in a group toward the door that we had come through.

My knees were bobbing, the leather of the seats squished when I moved, and my hands were leaving sweat prints on the large glass table. This was the same conference room that Carmen and Coach Hargrove had used when we negotiated my contract for the Lightning. This time, I was just as nervous, but for entirely different reasons.

I sat straighter when the door opened and Miss Romero and Coach walked in, followed by Dylan, the head of public relations, and John Savage, our attorney.

I stood and held out my right hand to greet them before we settled into chairs.

"First, Aaron how are you doing?" Carmen asked.

"As well as can be expected."

"What ended up happening?" Carmen looked as if she were genuinely interested, and not just placating me until she could ask when I was coming back.

"I have a seven-year-old daughter who will be coming to live with me, but I'm going to hire a nanny to help get her to and from school and stay with her when I'm gone."

"You sure you can handle both a child and this career?" Carmen raised one brow and waited for my answer.

"Absolutely. Ireland is my biological daughter, so there is no other answer than yes, I'm ready for this."

"If I may interrupt, what about the latest tabloid images?" Dylan asked.

"The woman in the picture was the family law attorney who was helping me get everything settled. I'm not sure how it became gossip or why someone thought we were together. That picture they are claiming was a 'tender moment' was when she patted my hand, reassuring me that we had this."

Dylan opened her laptop and started typing. "You know that the media is going to be hounding you, especially when they learn you have a seven-year-old daughter, right?"

"I know, but I'm ready for it. I'm not going to change my mind."

"Then let's get to the real topic at hand: your team needs you," Carmen jumped right in. "John is here to assist with any changes that we need to make to your contract."

"I'm ready to come back. For the first several games, I may ask that Ireland come with me, but after I hire a nanny that shouldn't be an issue. Her life has been turned upside down, so my main priority is to help her settle in and feel at home."

"I don't see any problem with her joining us, do you, Coach?" Carmen asked.

"Not as long as his head is in the game."

"Agreed," Carmen added. "Now, what did you want to add, Dylan?"

"I need us to decide how we want to present this to the public. Aaron, as you know, it is always best to get ahead of the media so we control the story. Have you given this any thought?"

"I'm thinking a quick press release or short conference,

no questions. I will see if Ireland wants to do it with me or if she wants me to do it alone. My private life shouldn't be up for public consumption, so we should make it clear that I am asking for my privacy in this matter. Are you okay with that?" I glanced over to Carmen because I wasn't stupid, I knew who my boss was and had no problem kissing ass.

"I think that sounds doable, do you agree, Dylan?"

"Absolutely, when would you like to schedule that for?" Dylan asked.

I thought about it for a second, it had been thirteen days since I had gotten the news about the accident. "I guess we could do it tomorrow."

Carmen waited for Dylan to answer. "Let's schedule it for tomorrow at ten a.m., but we need to decide what you're going to say and how much information to relay."

I had no clue how Ireland wanted me to refer to her. I pulled out my phone and sent Vivian a text and got worried when fifteen minutes had passed and I still hadn't received a reply.

VIVIAN

Slowly I took a step back and moved toward the other doorway. I scooted back even more when no one noticed me, and the small throng of people was almost off the basketball court.

Grabbing my phone from my pocket, I pulled up the Uber app and requested a car to meet me outside.

I needed to analyze what I had just seen. It wasn't that Aaron only had eyes for Ireland, it was strange people following and invading his privacy. Inviting reporters and photographers back into my life was something I promised myself that I would never deal with again. My hatred for them was genuine, and their tenacity was equal to that of a great white shark. I couldn't put myself in that position again.

I could still hear that damn photographer guy hollering questions at Aaron.

"Aaron, whose little girl?"

"Aaron, was that the mom, and is this your secret love child?"

"Aaron, what's her name? Introduce us."

When my phone dinged to alert me my driver was here, I headed for the car and got in. I only lived about ten minutes away, so I was home in no time.

My phone rang, dinged, and beeped, all from Aaron. He'd tried calling, texting, and even sending an email, but I wasn't in a mood to talk.

∼

I HAD ONLY BEEN HOME about thirty minutes before my doorbell rang. I peered through the peephole and was not too surprised to see Aaron and Ireland standing on my front porch.

"Open up, Vivian, I saw your shadow move past the window," Aaron said loudly, but not quite loud enough to be a yell.

With a huff, I opened the door, but there was no holding back my smile, because Aaron and Ireland were holding a box of pizza and pack of soda.

"We brought dinner," Ireland announced. "Where did you go? I looked everywhere, I was worried that there were more of those photographers and one grabbed you."

"Come on in." I held open the door to my small house and then led the way to the kitchen. I grabbed plates and napkins as well as cups. "Ice?"

"Not for me, the Cokes are cold." Aaron opened the box and pulled one out. "Here you go," he said as he handed one to Ireland and then set one down by a third chair for me. "What happened back there?"

"Too much. You know that I hate the press. I couldn't take it. I can't imagine how you live like that." I inhaled deeply and then went for a slice. "It isn't something I could live with. Your life is way too public for me." I tried to act nonchalant, as though I wasn't calling a halt to us, because I didn't want to alarm Ireland, but I needed him to know that this wasn't going any further. Feelings for him be damned, I wasn't doing that to myself.

"Tomorrow, I'm holding a press conference to let the media know a little of what is going on. After that, most of this should die down. I usually don't have much of a problem shopping or going out. Occasionally, people will interrupt me and ask for an autograph, but they leave me alone for the most part. I promise that this isn't the norm. It is simply reactions to what is going on. It will get back to normal, trust me, please." I locked eyes with Aaron, he was offering me a life raft, and I wanted so badly to take it.

I wanted to trust him.

I nodded, and he slipped one hand around the back of my neck and pulled me in for a quick kiss.

"Not at the table," Ireland moaned, and I cracked up laughing.

"So, Ireland, tomorrow do you want to talk with me?" Aaron asked.

"In front of people?" she asked.

"Yeah, it will be for the public," Aaron explained.

"No. Can I just stay with Vivian? She and I could work on my room." Ireland watched me and waited for my answer.

"I have to run into Sixes tomorrow and grab the books for payroll, but other than that, I'm free. So, I'm fine if Ireland stays with me. Maybe we can go get the paint?"

"Fine by me," Aaron agreed. "Do you want to pack a bag and stay over at my house?"

"Please, Vivian, please. Then tomorrow we can go shopping again. We got all the stuff from that barn store, but we still don't have a lot of clothes for me though."

"Not enough clothes?" I asked, shocked.

"Nope." Ireland mumbled as she shook her head, her mouth full of pizza.

"My god girl, you have more clothes than I do."

"Maybe you two need to go shopping and get clothes for Vivian too," Aaron added, but I ignored him. When he wasn't getting anything from me about his last statement, he changed the subject. "Why don't we get paint on the way home?" Aaron asked.

"Can we, please?" Ireland was super excited.

I MIXED a bag of play sand into clear glaze for the bottom of the ocean wall while Ireland pressed blue painter's tape around the baseboards. We had the television on and were waiting for Aaron to come on. There had already been a few teasers about big news from the NBA all-star.

"We interrupt this regularly scheduled show," Channel Four News announced. I avoided Channel Two like the plague thanks to Bitchasaurus, Haley Loles, but this wasn't something that would be picked up by national news anyway.

Ireland and I turned our attention to the screen.

"Thank you for coming today," Aaron announced. "First, I'd like to address the events from yesterday. A photographer stalked and harassed my family. I do not and will not accept any member of the press treating anyone like that, let alone my family." Aaron paused, and I was silently high fiving him. "Not only did it frighten a woman and a seven-year-old girl, but the police were called, and the single photographer cost taxpayers money because the police had to spend man-hours on him since he decided to break the law. Our fine men and women of Orlando Police Department have better things to do than babysit you. Please know that I will not tolerate any harassment of my family." Aaron paused, his eyes scanned the crowd.

"Two weeks ago, I received devastating news, friends of mine were in a car crash and the only survivor was their seven-year-old daughter, Ireland. I am now the legal guardian of Ireland. She will be living with me full-time as my daughter." Aaron took a long sip of water. "I have two people in my life. I love this seven-year-old girl who will be living with me. And I'm in love with the other woman who called me late one night and has been a part of my world ever since." Aaron peered into the camera and I swore he was talking straight to me. Holy cow, he loved me.

"He just said that he was in love with me, right?" I asked Ireland.

"Yep, he loves me too."

My phone dinged and I glanced at it.

STELLA: Holy shit, he loves you.

My phone dinged again.

MIKKI: You and Aaron, like really a couple? I'm so jealous and yet happy at the same time. Can I go to another game?

Piper: OMG, Vivian and Aaron sitting in a tree K-I-S-S-I-N-G.

OBVIOUSLY, everyone I knew was watching the press conference because my new messages were already over fifteen, so I flicked my phone to silent and tossed it aside to keep watching.

"I expect everyone to treat them with respect and afford them their privacy. I'm the ballplayer, not them. I'm your news story, not them. Let's get our ethics back on track."

Aaron stepped back from the podium as questions were shouted and then he turned and strode from the room.

I turned off the television and went back to sand, glaze, and a giant wall. I wasn't sure how long Ireland and I had been painting before we heard the garage door. I set my brush down and wiped my hands off on a rag.

"I'm going to go see Aaron real quick."

"Do you love him too?" Ireland asked.

"Yes I do."

"Are you two going to kiss?" Ireland made a kissy face.

"I hope so. I one hundred percent hope so."

As I turned for her door, Aaron was already there, grinning. I didn't walk, I leapt into his arms.

"I love you too."

"Good, because I think I fell in love with you the night you became my midnight call girl."

EPILOGUE

IRELAND

ne year later . . .

I PULLED on my favorite jean shorts that had a ruffle around the legs made of Orlando-Lightning-printed fabric. Then I dug through my drawers until I found the dark blue T-shirt that said Sixes and headed out of my room.

"How do I look?" I twirled in front of Vivian and Aaron for their opinion. I couldn't hide my smile when Vivian started laughing, since that was the reaction I was going for.

"Aren't you absolutely adorable? Is Sixes going to become a sports place?" Vivian asked.

I nodded. "*Mm-hmm.* It should be, or at least you need to make a sports wall. I can help if you need me to. I loved decorating my room."

"That's definitely a possibility." Vivian pulled me into her arms and gave me one of her huge hugs.

"You don't care if I wear this, do you?" I glanced over at Aaron, who was in a suit.

"Today is your day, you can wear whatever you want," he assured me. "We are just meeting the judge in his chambers."

"Like what you and I did when you brought me here?"

"Exactly like that. Now, tell me, how do I look?" Aaron twirled just like I had done.

"Handsome," Vivian said before I could say anything.

"You look so pretty, Vivian." I rubbed my fingers along the silkiness of her dress. "This looks good on you, but I don't like dresses."

"That's okay, you look pretty just the way you are."

"All right, you two, let's go," Aaron said as I turned for the doorway that led to the garage.

I raced to his car because I was so excited and climbed into the backseat. It didn't take too long, like eight songs or so, before we arrived at the courthouse.

As we walked up the marble stairs, people stopped and stared. This was the norm since Aaron was famous. I clasped on to Vivian and Aaron's hands as we finally reached the judge's office. When the door opened, I gulped. Everything in the room was dark and had a funny smell.

"Ugh, what's that smell?" I asked Vivian.

She giggled, "Shhh, it's called Liniment."

"What is lemmament for, cause it stinks."

"Shhh." She leaned over and whispered in my ear. "Older people use it on their achy muscles, it is supposed to help."

"I never want to be old if I have to use that."

"I don't blame you," a female voice said from behind me.

"Rut ro raggy," I said in my best Scooby-Doo impression.

The woman in the long black gown smiled. "Hello, I'm Judge Temperance Olson. Today is a busy day for you three, isn't it?" she asked me.

"Yep."

"Well, let's get started." Judge Olson moved around her desk and took a seat. "Let's make sure we are all on the same page. Mr. Skkye, you and Ms. Haines wish to marry, is that correct?"

"Yes," I answered for them. I was too excited.

The judge gave me a wide smile as Aaron and Vivian also said yes. "And you, Ireland, you want Aaron and Vivian to adopt you?"

"Well, just Vivian since I'm already Aaron's," I explained. Aaron's big hand squeezed mine.

The judge stood and came around to where we were. "Are you both ready?"

"Ready," Vivian agreed.

"Very well, do you have rings?" Aaron handed two rings over to the judge.

"Please face each other. Today, you enter as individuals, but you will leave here as husband and wife, blending your lives and beginning the story of your life together, which is yours to write. And Ireland, are you excited to be a part of their story?"

"Yes." I nodded.

"Please place the ring on each other's finger but don't push it over the knuckle." The judge waited as Vivian and Aaron did as asked. Then she asked them to tell each other they were giving a ring. I thought that part was stupid, because even I could see they were giving each other a ring.

"Do you, Aaron, take Vivian to be your lawful wedded wife, to have and to hold from this day forward, for better, for worse, for richer, for poorer, standing by her through sickness and health, through good times and bad, for as long as you both shall live?"

"I do." Aaron's voice was firm as he looked at Vivian, who was smiling wide. He pushed the ring onto her finger.

"And, Vivian, do you take Aaron to be your lawful wedded husband, to have and to hold from this day forward, for better, for worse, for richer, for poorer, standing by him through sickness and health, through good times and bad, for as long as you both shall live?"

"I do," Vivian announced as she pushed the ring onto Aaron's finger.

"By the power vested in me by the State of Florida, I now pronounce you husband and wife. You may kiss your bride." When the judge said that, I closed my eyes, because I didn't want to see them kissing. They did that a lot.

"Now, Ireland, it's your turn," Judge Olson announced.

"Do I have to say all of that stuff?" Everyone laughed, but I didn't think it was funny because none of that stuff they had just said made sense to me.

"Of course not, this is the easy part." The judge moved around her desk and took a seat again. I sat in the middle chair with Vivian and Aaron on either side of me as we faced her desk. "Ireland, do you want to be adopted by Vivian and Aaron?"

"Yes please. I would also like to make Lacy my middle name so I can have Skkye as my last, okay?"

"I can do that for you," the judge promised. "Vivian and Aaron, I need you to sign these papers." I watched as they both signed. "Very good. Once again, I'm excited to announce that the three of you are a family. Ireland, do you have anything you want to say?"

"Can I now call you Mom and Dad?" The answer they gave me was to pull me into a hug that was so tight I could barely breathe. Vivian kissed my face all over. "Hey, you were just kissing him with tongue, he probably licked your lips, gross. Don't be kissing me now." Ireland wiped her face.

When we left the judge's office, we headed toward the front doors but then stopped before pushing them open.

"Are you ready, Ireland?" Aaron asked, and I nodded. We walked out of the courthouse and photographers were all around snapping pictures. The three of us walked up to a podium. "Let me begin by thanking you all for being here. I'm hoping that by having this conference you all will learn the truth here and now from my mouth and will leave us alone in regards to our personal lives. I would like to introduce you to my wife—" Aaron said, and all of the reporters started shouting questions, but Aaron ignored them. "My wife, Vivian. And this is our daughter, Ireland. If you will excuse us now, we have a reception to get to."

We walked into Sixes, and I froze in awe.

"Surprise," people shouted.

"Ireland!" My friends Bee, Harlow, and Gianna raced up to me.

"My mom said that you can call her Aunt Sophie, and I'm like your cousin now," Harlow announced.

"Then that makes her my cousin too, since we're cousins," Bee added.

"Oh, you fabulous diva, did you dress yourself? Turn around, let ole Ringo take a look at this concoction." I turned for Ringo. He was a friend of my mom's, and he was a guy but liked to dress up like a girl and sing. He was funny. "I do believe we have our next fashionista in the making."

I turned in a circle and took in everything around me—all the people, the badges, helmets, and Dad's jersey from when the Lightning won the season finals last year. Home, this was home.

––––––––––––

The Iron Orchids story continues...

Ever since Piper became the first female motorcycle deputy, Orange County has been busy. Now, there's two. A new edition to the Iron Orchids—meet Sadie, the newest deputy to join in **Sadie, Doctor Accident**. Tap on the title to purchase or **Read for FREE with your Kindle Unlimited membership**.

Continue flipping the pages in this book for a sneak peek of Sadie, Doctor Accident and to find a list of all of my books including those included in Kindle Unlimited.

NOW AVAILABLE

NEW RELEASE
Kat, Knight Watch

Kat joins Sadie, Bridget, Piper, and the gang of motorcycle deputies in their quest to keep the streets of Orange County safe. Tap on the title to purchase or **Read for FREE with your Kindle Unlimited membership.**.

PREORDER
Ringo, Slippery Banana - 08/11/2020

Ringo is Here! Ringo gets his own book. Available now on Preorder.

BINGE READ ME

READ FOR FREE WITH YOUR KINDLE UNLIMITED MEMBERSHIP

Suggested Reading Order

ORIGINAL IRON ORCHIDS, BOOKS 1 THROUGH 7
TAP THE LINKS TO FIND EACH TITLE

Ariel, Always Enough - Book 1
Sophie, Almost Mine - Book 2
Katy, My Impact - Book 3
Leo, Kiss Often - Book 4
Stella, Until You - Book 5
Vivian, Midnight Call Girl - Book 6
Ringo, Slippery Banana - Book 7

IRON ORCHIDS—BADGES SERIES, BOOKS 8 THROUGH 11

You met some of them in the Iron Orchids. Now these women motorcycle officers will ride into your heart.

Sadie, Doctor Accident - Book 8
Bridget, Federal Protection - Book 9

Piper, Unlikely Outlaw - Book 10
Kat, Knight Watch - Book 11 (New Release)

IRON LADIES, BOOKS 1 AND 2

A whisper network of women. Women who help the wives of controlling men. You don't want to cross these ladies.

Adeline, Getting Even - Book 1
Sunday, Sweet Vengeance - Book 2

IRON HORSE, BOOKS 1 THROUGH 3

The love stories of three sisters who struggle to run a cattle ranch and to prove the strongest cowboys can be a girl.

London, Is Falling - Book 1
Paris, In Love - Book 2
Holland, At War - Book 3

BOX SET MADNESS

READ FOR FREE WITH YOUR KINDLE UNLIMITED MEMBERSHIP

IRON ORCHIDS COLLECTION
TAP THE LINKS TO FIND EACH TITLE

Iron Orchids, Box Set 1 - Ariel, Always Enough and *Sophie, Almost Mine*
Iron Orchids, Box Set 2 - Katy, My Impact and *Leo, Kiss Often*
Iron Orchids, Box Set 3 - Stella, Until You and *Christine, The Stars*

IRON HORSE COLLECTION

Iron Horse Box Set - London, Is Falling, Paris, In Love and *Holland, At War*

BOOK 8, IRON ORCHIDS

Chapter 1 - Sadie

*D*amn, *I made this shit look good.*

I stared at myself in the mirror for what had to be the tenth time this morning, making sure that my pins were perfect and my shirt was pressed. The only things that weren't sexy were the boots, but hey, I didn't mind them, since they were part of the standard uniform of all motorcycle deputies. Who would have ever guessed that I, Sadie Kathryn Lazar, would become a motorcycle deputy? I still got butterflies in my stomach just thinking about it. I mean . . . why wouldn't I? I was getting ready to roll out on two wheels of county-owned property, and it would be up to me to save the people of Orange County, Florida from danger. Okay, more often than not I was saving them from their own stupidity, and I wasn't doing it alone, but whatever. There were other deputies and city police officers and state troopers, but I was part of that team. I was twenty-eight fucking years old, and even though I wasn't a kid any longer, this was a lot of responsibility. A lot of pressure.

I grew up watching *Cops* with my daddy. I was all about *bad boys, bad boys, whatcha gonna do* thanks to that show, and I never wavered from my career choice.

My ten-minute warning alarm signaled it was time for me to get my ass in gear. After sliding my gun into its holster, I grabbed my helmet and marched out of my small duplex. I opened the door to my tiny garage, which was truly meant for storage, and rolled out my motorcycle before reporting in to dispatch.

"Thirteen twenty-two, ten-eight."

"Orange County copies. 05:57 hours." Dispatch confirmed that I was logged in and on duty.

I fired the engine on my bike and then rolled back on the throttle. To many, the roar of the engine might as well have been a foreign language, but to me, it was my native tongue.

As the early morning sun warmed my cheeks and the wind whipped against me, I hummed and maneuvered through the rush-hour traffic. It wasn't even ten minutes after beginning my shift that my call signal rang out across the radio.

"Thirteen twenty-two."

"Thirteen twenty-two, go ahead."

"Are you available to support a search at Mills and Colonial?"

"Ten-four, show me fifty-one, be there in under five." After letting dispatch know that I was on my way and less than five minutes out, I upped my speed, only slowing when I spotted the three deputy vehicles along a side road. "Hey, what's going on?" I asked Colton. The guy had been on the force about as long as I had.

"Hey, Sadie, this is one of those stories that is totally *Cops* worthy."

"Oh, do tell."

"It seems that Wanda"—he pointed to a tall woman in

gold stilettos and a catsuit (the pleather kind, not the furry kind)—"and her best friend Pammy are no longer best friends."

"Why?" I asked with all the fake concern I could muster, and Colton nodded with his own fake concern for their friendship.

"Wanda believes that Pammy stole her client."

"Well, that isn't a very best friend-like thing to do, is it?"

"Nope. Not at all." Colton was clearly trying to keep himself from laughing.

"Apparently, his name is John, and he's a very loyal . . . client." Colton raised an eyebrow.

"It's six o'clock in the fucking morning. If that doesn't say loyal, I don't know what does. So, why the sudden change of heart from our friend John the Client?"

"Oh." Colton finally lost it and let out a chuckle. "I'll let them tell you. I don't want to deprive you of any of the joy." Colton gave me a knowing grin and I shook my head as I flipped him off and made my way over to the two women.

I walked over. "Oh, good, missy, you need to arrest her. She's a thief."

"I ain't no thief, I'm a hooker." I looked over my shoulder to Colton, who had moved to stand with Dan and Enzo. All three were watching me with bored expressions. I knew better, and would pay each one of them back for this nonsense. Three male deputies, and they called me.

"Ladies, since the dispute has to do with business, this is actually a civil case and not criminal. You need to get an attorney and sue through the courts. Perhaps you can even try to get loss of income." Yeah, I said that last part with a straight face, looking to all the world like nothing more than a helpful officer handing out helpful advice.

"Wanda, I ain't taking no Johns from you," Pammy said. "I'm gonna be truthful, okay? I stole some of your Oxys. But, girl, you got so many from that guy you blew, you didn't even miss none."

I wanted to groan. Fuck, I needed to do a search.

"Okay, ladies," I said as I pulled out black plastic gloves. "I'm going to need you to step away from each other. If you could please face the car."

"What you doing, bitch? You ain't arresting her, she's my best friend." Wanda, who just seconds ago was claiming that they were no longer friends, looked ready to fight for said friendship.

"Ma'am, I'm going to need for you to step back unless you would like to wait in the back of one of those patrol cars." Being called a bitch was my official breaking point. For a second, I thought she was going to argue, but then Enzo opened the door for her and she quickstepped back four or five paces. Pammy didn't bother to argue as she assumed the position and pressed her palms flat.

Between the two women, I found seven Oxycontin and a few rocks of heroin, so off to the station they went...

Keep reading **Sadie, Doctor Accident**

A WORD FROM DANIELLE

*T*hank you for picking up my book. It doesn't matter whether you have read one book of ten written by me, they all have some commonalities to them:

Strong women with attitude.

Alpha heroes who love them anyway.

And a strong bond of friendship that we all need in our lives.

The Iron Orchids, books 1 through 6, were my original series of romance novels. Each book can be read as a stand-alone. What connects the stories are the fact the same people appear and eventually each gets their own Happily Ever After.

So if you've read one then you are probably dying to read about the rest of the brothers and their missing cousin.

Read on to find sneak peeks from some of the books along with my suggested reading order.

Thank you again - Dani

FIND ME

Website: www.daniellenorman.com

Official Iron Orchids Reading Group : www.daniellenor-man.com/group

Sign up for Danielle's Newsletter and stay in the know
Newsletter: www.daniellenorman.com/news

Go to your App Store and download the app called Danielle Norman or visit
app.daniellenorman.com to download from the internet.

MEET DANIELLE

*D*anielle began her career as a children's author where her books earned acclaim on several lists for bestselling author. Not to mention Library Guild awards and STEM award author of the year.

BUT HER BELIEFS have always been that vodka, high heels, and a well-spoken F-word could solve almost any problem. Unfortunately those things aren't the foundation for kids books. So, she switched her name (Danielle is her middle name, Norman is her husband) to protect the innocent and started writing romance, nothing like strong women, hot men, and steamy action.

ALSO BY DANIELLE

BOOKS BY STELLA LANG

Stella Lang is the husband and wife writing duo of
Rusty and Danielle Norman.

When reading books by Stella Lang you can always
count on strong women, alpha men, hot sex (lots of
hot sex), sarcasm, and a happily ever after that will
curl your toes.

Stella Lang began as a sarcastic heroine in books by
Danielle Norman.

Get your copy of ***Hard Blow***, Book 1 of the Orlando Suns
series. Read for Free with your Kindle Unlimited
membership.

THANK YOU

It may take a village to raise a child but it takes a village, a tribe, and a gang to get a book out.

Special thanks to Ashley who still puts up with me and my ever revolving idiosyncrasies.

Thank you Taryn for your proofreading excellence.

Thank you Theresa, Oxford Comma Editing for the final set of eyes.

As always Peggy, my brainstormer, first eyes, and swag bag stuffer.

And Finally to the Iron Orchids, you are the best gang ever.

DANIELLE NORMAN

heers,
Dani

Made in the USA
Columbia, SC
11 June 2020